HEARTICAL

MEGAN AHASIC

HEARTICAL

READERSMAGNET, LLC

Heartical
Copyright © 2017 by Megan Ahasic

Published in the United States of America
ISBN Paperback: 978-1-947765-06-1
ISBN eBook: 978-1-947765-07-8

All rights reserved. No part of this publication may be reproduced, stored in a retrieval system or transmitted in any way by any means, electronic, mechanical, photocopy, recording or otherwise without the prior permission of the author except as provided by USA copyright law.

The opinions expressed by the author are not necessarily those of ReadersMagnet, LLC.

ReadersMagnet, LLC
80 Broad Street, 5th & 6th Floors Finance District | New York City, NY 10004 USA
1.646.880.9760 | www.readersmagnet.com

Book design copyright © 2017 by ReadersMagnet, LLC. All rights reserved.
Cover design by Ericka Walker
Interior design by Shieldon Watson

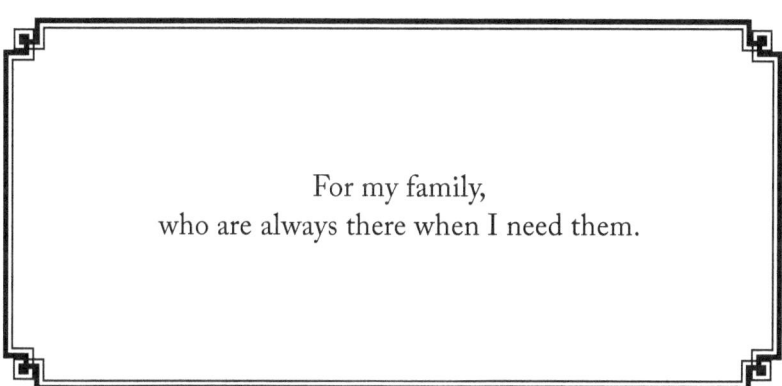

For my family,
who are always there when I need them.

Acknowledgments

I would like to thank my Lord and Savior for being faithful and true; my family for putting up with me and being there for me every step of the way; to the real life tide swooner, Brian Campbell, for letting me use his word "heartical" and bend it to my story; all the great teachers I've had for encouraging me; and my coworkers at McDonald's who believed in me.

Prologue

Behind Oceanrise Condominiums
Sarasota, Florida

A child walked along the sidewalk by the ocean. His strides were short but labored. His head was down, his shoulders hunched, his back bent. He cast his teal eyes to the ground, his reddish brown hair ruffled by a gentle breeze. He'd spent his first night sleeping in the bushes last night and had made sure he was not seen by a single soul. He stepped onto one of the docks spanning the coast and continued his journey. At the edge of the dock, he sat down and dangled his feet over the side. His legs swung back and forth as he faced the water, fixing his surroundings with an unseeing stare. His vacant eyes roamed over the small inlet and landed on the shore across the water. In between these two shores, the Gulf of Mexico's dark green water sparkled. The waves lapped against the dock posts, making a soft *plunking* sound. Every now and then, he heard splashing as fish jumped out of the water.

Normally, the beautiful sight would have drawn the boy's attention, but not today. He folded his arms against his chest and rocked himself. His eyes remained wide and distant. He smacked his lips, his tongue clicking against his teeth.

In the water, a gleam of silver broke through the surface and flashed through the air. It traveled upward and arced back down. The dolphin came up, leapt again, and twisted the top half of his body. A grin was on his face as he glanced about, sailing through the air in freefall. He spotted a boy all alone on the dock. Hmmm, thought the dolphin, this could be interesting. He swam toward the boy.

The boy, meanwhile, was far away. He traveled back in his mind to yesterday morning.

It started off happily enough. Serene seams of sunshine filtered down from between the peach colored clouds. A little of his joy was lost in sadness, however, for this was the day vacation ended. He and his parents were getting ready to drive back to their home in Rhode Island after a fun-filled summer trip to Florida. The boy flicked a longing gaze up at their fifth floor condo at Oceanrise as they were loading the car. Next summer, maybe we'll get to go for a carriage ride, he thought, wishing there had been time to take the horse and carriage tour of Siesta Key. Once the luggage was loaded, his mother drove down to the front office and parked along the nearby curb. The office was located to their right, only a few feet shy of the street entrance to Midnight Pass Road.

His dad got out of the van to return their condo keys. His mother had just picked up the last of their mail and was rifling through it. The boy got out behind his dad. His father watched him and said, "You coming in with me, buddy?"

The boy nodded, grabbed his trusty backpack, and slid the back door shut. He turned toward his dad.

"Do you really need to take that backpack in with you? We'll only be in there a few seconds," his father said.

"But all my treasures are in here," the boy replied.

"Okay." As they headed up the sidewalk, his dad stopped for a moment. With a devious twinkle in his eye, he took off one of his wrist bands and held it out to his son. "Here, buddy, you can have this to add to your treasures."

The boy's eyes lit up. "Really?"

His father nodded and placed it in his hand. "Promise me you'll take good care of it. That's my favorite wrist band."

"I promise."

His father grinned, and they continued into the office. A moment later they emerged.

"Roger," called the boy's mother, "come here."

Roger looked at her, noting her pale face. She was holding a piece of mail and shaking. "What is it, Christina?"

"Just get over here now," she said.

"Wait here, son," Roger said.

The boy remained on the sidewalk beside the green van. His dad had just stepped in front of the van, when his mom began whispering to him. They became animated and excited, gesturing wildly. His mother was waving a piece of paper around, a letter, and then she handed it to his father. His dad scanned it, a slow smile forming on his face. He carefully slid the letter into the envelope, handed it back to her, and said something his son could not hear. Maybe we won the lottery, the boy thought. This was the only thing he could think of that would make them jump around like that. They both sprang forward into an embrace. His father pulled away and pointed at him. His mother shook her head then shrugged.

He was about to go to them, but his dad said, "Stay there, Brian. It'll just be a minute. Okay, sailor?"

"Okay, Dad."

Brian watched their discussion with rapidly growing boredom. Finally, he looked away. By chance, his glance happened to land on the street in front of the entrance. As he watched, a gray Lincoln barreled down Midnight Pass. Wow, that guy's going fast, Brian thought. He could get a ticket. The Lincoln's engine roared, overtaxed. The smell of burning oil wafted through the air. Smoke crawled out from under the hood. Brian gasped as the car lurched sideways and angled toward the curb at the edge of the entrance. The car was flying when it hopped the curb, eating up the short distance between the entranceway and his parents' van. The car was headed right for his parents. Brian tried to cry out, but his throat had gone dry. Mom, Dad, move, he thought, hoping he'd said it aloud. For a moment, he thought he had, because they both turned toward the car. They had heard its brakes squealing.

The driver of the Lincoln swerved. The tires screeched as the driver jerked the wheel, trying to avoid a collision. Brian was relieved for a moment. Then he saw how close the car was coming to the van. His parents opened their mouths, but they were stunned into silence as the car sideswiped them. They were stuck between the two cars for an instant, their legs pinned in a vice of fiber glass and steel. The guy steered wildly to the right, cutting a crude U-turn. He barely missed smashing into a light pole. The car boomed and rattled as its wheels slammed back onto the highway. Brian watched as his parents slipped backward up the hood of the van then crumpled down the front of it. His legs buckled, and he landed hard on his knees, scraping them on the rough-grooved sidewalk. His backpack thudded to the ground beside him. Somehow the solid sound of his treasures hitting the ground was what broke the line between denial and reality.

The letter his mother had been holding flew out of her hand on impact and floated under the van, caught in the breeze. It came out on the other side, landing in a puddle of water near the rear tire. Dazed, Brian reached out toward it. As his fingers touched the envelope, the early morning sky above turned gray. The peach color of the clouds faded to gray-brown as they drew together and blocked out the sun. Brian curled his fingers around the edge of the envelope and lifted it just as rain burst from overhead. Distracted, he slipped the letter into his backpack. Behind him, a man came out of the office. He heard the man exclaim something then run back inside. Brian wanted to go to his parents, but he was afraid of what he would see. A few moments later, he heard sirens approaching.

A spray of water hit him, startling him back to the present. He looked out at the water and saw a dolphin swimming nearby.

Orphans of the Sea

The coastal waters were calm for the morning service. Representatives of the largest sea animals were all gathered. One entire dolphin pod was to lead the ceremony. A dolphin named Mari was just about to slip into a good spot at the back of the line, certain that the rest of his pod wouldn't want him in front, especially their leader, Alpha dolphin. Alpha sought him out, however.

"Mari, you will stay here during the ceremony." He gestured to a spot right up front.

Why, Mari wondered. He gawked as everyone moved to make way for him. That was odd. No one had ever treated him with such respect; even this forlorn deference was new to him. As he listened to Alpha's speech, it occurred to him that he had never heard Alpha sound so noble.

"We are gathered here, as you all know by now, to commemorate the memory of our beloved Maiden of the Sea. She was one of the best rulers these oceans have ever seen, a true legend. I only wish an heir could be found. She left us with many great legacies. And, of course, our own Mari was one of them," he said, nodding to Mari, who was still confused.

He'd never heard anything like that about himself. Alpha finished the eulogy. They all bowed their heads in grief and respect. Then it was over. As they were leaving, Mari found Alpha.

"Alpha, what did you mean that I'm one of her legacies?"

Alpha shook his head. "No questions. It is a day of mourning."

Mari knew it. There would be no answers, not today and not tomorrow. He was almost as depressed by this as he was by the sea queen's death. To cheer himself up, he decided to cruise the inlet behind Oceanrise Condominiums and play. As he did flips, trying to touch the morning's pale blue sky, he happened to look over at the shore.

His gaze fell on a huddled form at one of the boat docks. Mari realized it was a child hunched over the harbor. He looked the boy over thoroughly, noticing his shirt and shorts. His turquoise shirt had some clouds, a bright yellow sun, two dark yellow sand dunes, and a palm tree on it. His yellow shorts were actually swimming trunks with two words scrawled down the sides in blue. One word was *Aloha,* and the other was *Rules.* Despite the kid's vacation-type clothing, he was crying. Some force he could not explain drew Mari to this melancholy creature.

He always enjoyed being close to the shore, anyway, showing off when other dolphins were nearby, because they were afraid to get this close. Their main rule was that no land creature was to be trusted in the ocean ecosystem. They were afraid of humans, and shore was where those awful human beings dwelled. Mari rebelled against their rules and superstitious cautions, because none of them had ever really accepted him into their hearts. Oh sure, they looked out for him, but they looked upon him with an echoing dolphin groan as a burden to their clan. Pft, what a bunch of cowards. Why should they fear all humans, he thought. Most of them weren't bad. And, he wondered, why should my fellow dolphins fear me?

They seemed to fear him because, somehow, he was different, just as they feared humans because of their land-dwelling differences. For some reason, they had unconsciously put Mari in the same class as the land creatures and looked upon him with mistrust. Consequently, he had no friends or playmates. Looking at the boy, Mari was briefly reminded of another human face, one with wavy orange hair and teal eyes. It was the Maiden of the Sea, the ocean queen, now passed on.

When Mari reached the dock, a wave of emotion hit him deep inside and receded like the tide, drawing his own feelings out. He let out a gasp. His heart pounded, and he was warm all over. For a moment, he was nauseated, but it passed quickly. This child, he thought. I want to protect him. No one in his pod had ever made him feel this way. The boy had his arms crossed over his chest as if to hold himself together. He looked young, maybe eight or nine. Mari wasn't sure because the way humans aged was a mystery to him. The boy shivered, though it wasn't cold outside.

"Hey, kid? What's wrong?" Mari asked. He shifted uncomfortably, not really expecting a reply from the kid. Most humans could not speak or understand dolphin vernacular.

The boy lifted his head, whipped it around, then stared at Mari with surprise. "What? D-did you say t-that, dolphin?" he stammered. His pleasant little voice, soft and high, was almost like laughter. He jumped and stood up full. His eyes never left Mari's.

"Uh-huh." Mari smiled.

"Whoa," the kid cried, neck swiveling to look at his companion from different angles.

"Hi. My name's Mari. What's yours?"

"I-I…I'm Brian." He wore a coming-out-of-a-daze expression, and his voice had a dreamy and delighted quality. He sat back down.

"Nice to meet ya, uh, Brian."

"Likewise," the kid said with a grin.

"What's that mean?" Mari anxiously moved his fluke up and down under the water, which was habitual for him when nervous or confused. What confounding creatures these are, he mused.

"It means that I'm glad to meet you, too." Brian said this with a great deal of flair, raising his eyebrows and lowering them automatically, eyes crinkling up as he did so, jaw quivering and moving up and down.

"Oh. So, you from around here?"

"Siesta Key? No. My parents and I came down for vacation." He stopped speaking and sobbed.

Okay, now what, Mari wondered. "I'm sorry. Listen, I didn't mean to offend you, kid."

"Nah, it's all right," he said, his voice choked with tears. "I'm just sad because my, my parents d-died yesterday morning."

Mari's eyes went wide, and he let out a sympathetic sigh. Brian scooted to the edge of the dock. Mari nuzzled his face with the edge of what these creatures considered his nose or snout. Brian's skin was smooth and chilled, like the ocean water at night. The boy closed his eyes and gripped the end of Mari's snout with his small hand. He stroked the tip with his little fingers. Wow, they died, Mari thought. A pang rose in his chest. It reminded him that he also had no parents. He really didn't know if they died or got lost somewhere as the pod was traveling during the years before settling near Florida; but before he was old enough to remember them, they were gone. And because of that, death was something he could be sympathetic toward but not comprehend.

"How'd they die?"

"Car accident," the boy explained briskly. It sounded as if he was trying to brush it off, but his downcast eyes made all the difference. He frowned, brows knit up.

Mari's eyes softened. "Why aren't you with the rest of your family, then?"

"Mom and Dad were the only family I had left," he whispered.

"Oh." Mari paused, not sure what to say.

The boy sniffed and began sobbing again. Mari shifted his eyes away then slid them back to the kid. He was startled when the boy spoke again.

"Mom had a special saying for moments like these," Brian added, sniffling.

"What moments?"

"The down moments," he said. "She said they are beautiful because they are part of the heartical."

"Part of the what?" Mari asked. I don't think there's anything beautiful about this, he decided.

"Heartical. She defined this as the totality of our life experience. She said that it stood for the full range of emotional and physical events that make up an individual's existence."

"Why would she think that's beautiful?"

"Because she thought our very existence is beautiful with its ups and downs. And she told me that the beauty is in all the things we learn because of that experience. These things make us who we are."

Mari was confused. "Was she saying that we need the down moments to be happy or something?"

Brian shook his head. "No. She said that the bad moments enhance our happiness by providing contrast. So our experience, good and bad, is part of an amazing process that continues throughout our lives. Heartical is the epitome of that process."

"Uh-huh," Mari said. "Your mom couldn't have thought of a simpler way to say all this?"

A ghost of a smile formed on the boy's face. "She was very complicated."

"No kidding," Mari said. "Are you stranded here, then?"

"No, I just…have no home. I'm an orphan now."

Mari tried his best to think of a way to make the kid smile. He glanced about at the dark, green water surrounding him. An idea came to him. Mari looked shyly at Brian, whose eyes were blazing with emotion.

"Would you like to go for a ride on my back?" Mari thought that would make him feel better: human beings loved to ride things.

Brian's eyes grew large. He wiped absently at the tears on his face. "Are you sure?"

Mari grinned and said, "Climb aboard, sailor."

Brian drew in a harsh breath, taken aback. He called me sailor, he thought. He pushed the swarming memories of yesterday morning back to the corner of his mind. Mari peered at him as he recovered his composure. The boy got up, looked around, and threw his backpack into the bushes.

"Okay," he whispered. There was a hesitant eagerness on his face.

Mari laughed as Brian slipped onto his back and put his arms around him, his legs locking together just above Mari's tail fluke. When he hooked his fingers around Mari's dorsal fin, Mari carried him slowly around the inlet. The boy wasn't all that heavy, and the water, so warm and soothing and slick, carried most of his weight when they went under enough to cover him to mid-thigh. The dark green surface water was a dark teal underneath. The boy unclasped his legs and let them stretch out behind him above Mari's tail. At first, Mari worried he would fall, but he proved to be an excellent rider. It's like he's done this all his life, he mused. He decided it was time to head out to the open sea. Brian giggled with excitement as they rocketed off. He pulled himself up onto his knees on Mari's back. Then he let go of Mari's fin and thrust both his arms out wide. The biggest grin was stretched across his face, reflected in his magnificent ocean-colored eyes.

"Yee-ha," the child shrieked.

"Hold tight now, sailor."

Brian gripped him more securely, but not too tight. Mari dove straight down for a few feet, one eye glancing back to enjoy the boy's smile, and then he curved his body upward, the boy moving as one with him. All they saw when they surfaced was sea spray mixed with sky and water droplets. The boy began to slide backward but caught himself by clasping his legs underneath Mari. Mari relished the sounds they made as they broke through the water. They launched into the atmosphere with a big *whoosh-roar*.

Water fanned out in huge showers like a visible dash of wind. The sea's frothing foam was supple and warm against their skin. Brian slid forward as his legs stretched across Mari's back. They soared through the air in an arc and blasted back down, sending mists of water flying in all directions. The feeling of plunging toward the water was frightening, invigorating, and something that filled them with a desire for more. They hit the water hard but did not feel it. As they sank, the boy's legs slid to the left, and he nearly tumbled off, but Mari swerved to catch him. At last, he surfaced for air and blew his breath out through his blowhole. This caused an outbreak of laughter from Brian. Mari stared at him, bewildered.

"Man, it sounded like you ripped one," he explained through a gale of laughter.

Mari started to ask what he meant when he suddenly got it. He cracked up.

"Dude, if I had done that, I'd a ripped a hole in my shorts," Brian blurted out.

That got them both going again, and soon they were gasping for breath. The rest of the day was spent playing water tag. Toward evening, Mari dropped him off where he'd found him, aware that the boy would need to sleep soon. Dolphins didn't sleep as long as humans because they didn't have gills and had to surface for air. They could only take short naps to replenish their bodies. Brian waved at him as he walked off, looking thoroughly ridiculous in his drooping, wet clothes.

Mari suddenly longed to go with him. "Bye, sailor," he called.

"Goodbye, Mari. See you around." He hurried down the sidewalk.

As Mari watched him, he knew that the kid was contemplating the emptiness that came of not knowing where to turn. He sighed. The sky had turned gray without his realizing it. He saw Brian slip underneath the bush where his backpack was hidden.

Mari was reluctant to leave him alone and stayed for a while, idly staring at the shore. The wind picked up, and he noticed a blue and purple beach towel outlined in red floating on the air. He surveyed it until, to his astonishment, it stopped right next to the bush where his new friend slept. Suddenly, a translucent figure of a man appeared. He was holding the towel. He looked at Mari a moment, smiling, then bent into the bush with the towel. It came to him that the man was covering the kid with it, draping it over him like a blanket. Then the spirit was gone.

The way the spirit had turned to look at him weighed on Mari's mind. Could this be fate, he thought. He did not know if he believed in such a thing as destiny. He had, until then, been resigned to a semi-bearable life within his family, not considering that there may be other possibilities. With unease, he remembered the force that had drawn him to the boy. What was that? He knew that there was a creator of all things, called Lord or God, but he didn't really know Him. He was far removed from God's eye, at least that's what he thought. Just as he thought that surely, being a water creature, he was far removed from the world of land creatures.

However, he could literally feel a connection to each life force on the planet, for energy ran through all things. The vibrancy of every creature and inhabitant of earth flowed, passed through him.

Bizarre, Mari observed. I feel this connection, but I've never felt any connection to my parents. He had never known them. And he had always been curious as to why he was the only one to have lost both parents. The pod never spoke of his mother and father. Then there was this legacy of the maiden business that Alpha was so secretive about this morning. Every time he asked questions, the leaders of the pod, as well as everyone else, became still and silent. They didn't even bother being evasive: they just remained stoic until he turned away in frustration. I want some answers, he decided. Mari headed home to try asking about his parents again.

A Real Friend

Mari went to the spot where the pod gathered. As he swam up, some of his fellow dolphins eyed him with suspicion, surprise, and even contempt. Puzzled, he looked around. This was worse than usual. Many heads turned away, and some of them even turned fully around and flapped their flukes in his face, a serious insult in dolphin society. At last, a voice spoke out.

"What are you doing, Mari?" It was their leader.

"Huh? What's this all about?"

"We know that you approached a human boy. And worse, you were playing with it! Do you know how dangerous that is?" Alpha asked with a scowl.

Mari found this notion absurd, given that many dolphins served man by helping out the lost ships, and told him so. Alpha glowered at him.

"You know the rules."

"Yeah, but the maiden was also a human," Mari countered.

"Don't you dare speak of her. She wasn't like the other humans. She was special. Can't you see everyone's still upset about her passing? If you can afford to be so calm about that, then you can also afford to be more considerate."

"Come on, Alpha." Mari rolled his eyes.

"I can see that we don't understand one another. You refuse to change, so I have no choice," Alpha interrupted. "You've become a threat to us. We do not wish for you to call us your brethren anymore."

Mari looked at him, uncomprehending. Then horror bloomed in his eyes. His heart asked how they could do this to him. "Does this mean what I think it does?"

Alpha nodded. "Banishment. Get out of here!" His harsh voice cut into Mari.

As Mari turned to go, Alpha flew into his side, nudging him hard with his nose. Mari cried, because this was the mark of the deepest banishment. Alpha had tried to scar him, to brand him so that any other dolphin pod would recognize him as an outcast. This would let them know not to take him in. Now he had nothing left, all because he had approached a human. Mari was surprised at the amount of emotion he felt. He had always been a stranger, even within his own family, but now he realized just how alone he would truly be. The memory of their disapproving faces seared itself into his mind.

Their steely gazes burned a hole in his fluke as he swam off. Now he had no family, no one, except that boy. Maybe he would run into the kid again. He dared to hope that he had found a real friend.

He couldn't help wondering why all this had happened. Why did everything have to be so hard? And why was it always him who kept screwing things up? If this truly was destiny, then he wanted no part of it. His life had been bad enough before, so he didn't need help making it worse. What, he wondered, is the good of destiny if it constantly brings pain? After running his mind over these self-pitying platitudes, he thrust his fluke up and down swiftly and jetted off into the night, more uncertain than ever.

The next day he did indeed see the boy again. This time, he found Brian at Turtle Beach. It was a very desolate beach full of hills and sharp deposits of sea shells that most tourists ignored. The sand here was a darker brown, very grainy, and hotter than the finer white sands of Crescent and Sarasota beaches. Because the other beaches were so populated, he tended to swim near this one, so that he was free of the crowds. Other dolphins, however, preferred to roam near the more populated beaches. Why this was, he didn't know, especially given their considerable fear of humans. He greeted the boy. I wonder why he's here of all places, Mari thought. Brian still had the beach towel with him.

"Hey, Mari," he called.

"Aloha! Buddy! What's up?"

He looked confused for a second then figured it out. "You calling me that now?"

"Sure thing, sailor."

Mari winked at him. Humans always enjoyed that one. They thought it was cute and special and meaningful. Aloha grinned. Mari gathered that he liked the nickname. He also noticed that Aloha was still wearing the clothes he'd had on the night before, not that he minded. Those clothes were retro enough.

"Mari? Do you know how this beach towel got on me? It was just there when I woke up."

"Nope," he lied. He didn't know how to explain that a ghost had given it to him as a blanket. "Hey, why'd you come to this bland beach when the others are so much nicer?"

"I came here earlier to sleep. I wanted to leave before the people in the condos woke up."

"Oh."

"What brings you out here, Mari?"

"No reason, really. Wanna go for a swim?" Mari had never invited anyone to swim with him before, and he surprised himself by extending this invitation.

"Yeah. Just let me go shower first. Haven't showered in two days."

Mari tilted his head and eyed his friend curiously. Aloha ran off to the beach showers and scrubbed himself clean. Mari thought this might be a good idea, since some of these creatures had a tendency to pollute the oceans and environments surrounding them. Once he finished, Aloha raced toward the bluish-gray water, kicking up a lot of sand—and his sandals—as he did so. He ran barefoot into the water, splashing loudly. Mari jumped high as he neared and soaked him. Aloha sprayed him back. He echoed his approval, and they swam alongside each other for hours, resting every now and then. Mari had decided to take him to a place he did not often venture, a place called Eden, when he saw Aloha start to slow down. He stopped swimming. His eyes looked grainy. Slowly, his eyelids came down, covering half of his eyes.

"What? What is it?" Mari asked.

"I'm tired." He panted, breathing hard from exertion. His voice was muffled and unenergetic. This alarmed Mari.

"Hang on to my dorsal, little friend. I'll take you to shore," he said.

"Okay."

Aloha thanked him as he grabbed his fin. Mari nodded and swam toward shore. Aloha lurched forward when he stopped unexpectedly. Mari could see a long shadow under the water, and it was approaching with impressive speed. Maybe if I stop moving, he thought.

"Mari? Why ya stopping?"

"Don't move. I think there's a…"

The black-eyed, great white shark popped up in front of them at that exact moment. Mari froze. He knew he could probably give the great white quite a hassle on his own, but with the boy to protect, it looked bad. They were caught. He was about to tell Aloha to swim for shore, that he would hold the shark off, when something whizzed past him. Blue fabric flashed in front of his eye. He saw Aloha's fist land squarely on the shark's snout. He looked over at Aloha, who was glaring at the shark, not the least bit scared.

"Get outta here, you dumb shark," he yelled.

Much to their surprise, after a moment's stare down, the shark turned. Mari thought he was going to leave, but then he went under, once more coming at them. The dolphin shot forward so fast that Aloha slid off his back. Then he dove under, racing for the shark. The shark was so intent on Aloha that he didn't see Mari coming until it was too late. His snout hit home, ramming the shark right in the gills. The shark clamped his mouth closed in pain then slashed his tail fiercely from side to side, swimming away from them. Mari swam underneath Aloha and surfaced, allowing Aloha to grab hold of his dorsal as he hurried toward shore. He was a little perturbed. Great whites were not native to this area. They were more likely to be found around California. What was he doing here, Mari wondered.

Aloha embraced him when they arrived safely at the shore. "Mari?"

Mari looked at him affectionately, noticing the somber timbre in his voice. "Yes?"

"We're friends, right?"

"Yeah."

They stayed near shore and took it easy for the remainder of the afternoon. In the middle of the night, Mari took him back to the docks behind Oceanrise. Aloha crawled under another bush to sleep. Before Mari swam away, Aloha called to him.

"Mari, I'll meet you at Turtle Beach again tomorrow."

"See ya there," Mari agreed.

The next day, Aloha came to the beach for their play time. On this morning, however, he didn't look so well. He was pale and lacked energy. He stumbled over a hill toward the water, fell in the sand with a *thwack*, and tried to get up, but couldn't. Oh no, Mari thought.

"What's wrong?" he asked.

"I'm so hungry," Aloha murmured before he passed out.

Now, it had never occurred to Mari that the kid wasn't getting anything to eat. Of course, he realized as Aloha lay unconscious, he has no money, and that's why he is always wearing the same clothes. He watched his new—and only—friend, wishing he could help. But no one was around to help. Hope quickly returned, for soon another little boy came running over the sandy hills. He had a gray, black, and cream-colored dog in tow that looked like an unusually large Keeshond. The boy saw Aloha with his thin pink eyes and ran to him. The dog loped swiftly to Aloha's side. The dog's kid had some strange hair: lavender-colored in wavy spikes. But strange hair or not, he shook Aloha gently and peered at him as his dog watched with his eyeglass-marked eyes.

"Hey, kid. Get up." The stranger's voice was full of concern.

Aloha's eyelids fluttered and opened. "Huh? Who're you?" Aloha's voice was weak and congested, his expression dull and confused. He coughed a couple of times, and the dog licked his face. He smiled briefly at the mutt and stroked the side of its face.

"Huron," the kid stated, looking from his dog to Aloha. He seemed to be considering something.

"I'm Aloha."

"Aloha?" Huron said, wrinkling his brow. "What kind of name is that?"

"A good one," he replied, his voice still strained. His expression was not offended, however. Both the dog and Huron gazed at him, apparently trying to size up the situation.

Huron eyed Aloha cautiously. "What's wrong with you, anyway?"

"I haven't eaten in a few days."

Huron's eyes widened. "Oh. Well, here, you can have my lunch, then."

"Thanks."

"No problem." Huron handed him a paper sack. The dog sat between them.

Huron helped Aloha sit up, and Aloha scarfed down something called a peanut butter sandwich and a bag of potato chips, some pretzels, and a pudding cup, as well as a Coke. Mari knew what the last one was because he had seen a half-empty Coke bottle floating in the harbor one day. The boy looked much better after he had eaten. His color returned, and his eyes brightened. Aloha thanked Huron for the meal once more. Huron nodded, a trace of a smile forming on his face.

"Hey, Aloha?"

"Yeah?"

"How old are you?"

"Eight. You?"

"Ten."

"Wow. So, what's your dog's name?" Aloha petted the dog in question.

"Tails, and he's not a dog, not really. He's a wolf."

Aloha's eyes widened, and he murmured an amazed reply that Mari was too busy thinking to hear. Ten, Mari thought, incredulous. That boy was shorter than Aloha.

"Hey, wanna come to my house and spend the night?" Huron was saying when Mari tuned back in to their conversation.

"Okay."

Aloha hadn't hesitated for a second. Mari had to admit that he felt abandoned. This was his first friend, after all. The boys hurried off together. Aloha waved to Mari and smiled over his shoulder as he left. Mari waved back with one fin, grateful that he hadn't been forgotten about. He followed the boys and Tails from the water and got lucky. Huron's family lived in a house along the beach, and he could see it from the water. The house was light brown in color and had dark brown shingles on the roof. Huron ran up to his mother upon their arrival and promptly asked if Aloha could spend the night. She had light blue hair and dark blue eyes and was standing next to a man with dark purple hair and bright pink eyes. She glanced at Aloha, who looked up at her bashfully.

"All right. Hello, Aloha."

"Hi, madam," he said grandly, his eyes going to the ground after meeting her gaze.

There was a brief but instantaneous agony that flashed through Aloha's eyes. Huron's mother put a consoling hand on his shoulder for a moment, even when he flashed a winning smile back at her. Tails began licking Aloha's hand, and Huron's mom patted the mutt's head with soft strokes.

As the afternoon wore on, Mari nearly went out of his mind with boredom watching the two play checkers and chess for hours at a patio table on the deck. The sliding glass door opened, and someone else came out. A taller, older boy emerged that also had strange hair. His hair was dark blue, and his eyes were a shade of blue that appeared almost black. He had the lean muscle of adolescence and moved with long, confident strides. His eyes were alive with happiness. The teenager walked up to Huron, ruffled his hair, scratched Tails behind one ear during which time the mutt looked extremely pleased, and gave his mom a big hug. Then he noticed Aloha. He grinned and held out his hand. Aloha returned his smile and shook his hand.

"Hey, dude. I'm Jake. Jake Horato."

"I'm Aloha."

"Cool threads, man." Jake continued to compliment him as he pushed a few loose strands of hair back into place. Mari smiled, liking this kid.

"Thanks. How old are you, Jake?"

"Fifteen."

Aloha gaped. "Wow, you're old. I'm only eight."

"Thanks. Hey, I know. Let's go surfing," Jake suggested.

"Yeah," Huron shouted. The kid obviously looked up to his brother. Aloha's eyes wavered with envy. He had always wanted a brother.

"I don't know how to surf," Aloha admitted.

"We'll show you."

"What if I'm no good?" he asked.

Huron interjected, "You'll be fine. We haven't been surfing all our lives, you know. We only moved here a year ago from Minnesota."

"Really? I've never been to Minnesota. Is it pretty there?"

"Oh yeah," Jake cut in. "Huron loved it there, because he enjoyed exploring the woods near our house."

"Oh, cool. So why'd you guys move?" Aloha inquired.

Huron hesitated. At last, he confessed, "Well, I got bullied a lot."

"Why were people picking on you?" Aloha asked.

"Because I'm small, and because I'm smart."

Curious, Aloha said, "What'd they do to you?"

Huron lowered his eyes. At last, he whispered, "One of them lit my shirt on fire while I was on the bus. He wasn't supposed to have a lighter with him, but he did."

Aloha gaped. "And this kid was the same age as you?"

"Yeah," Huron replied softly.

Aloha balked at the idea. "What a psycho."

"Yeah, third grade is tough nowadays," Jake added.

Aloha whistled. "I guess."

Huron blushed and looked away. Jake patted his shoulder and said, "Dude, it's nothing to be ashamed of, Huron."

Huron said nothing. Aloha added, "If it makes you feel any better, someone once chucked a spoonful of peaches at me during lunch."

Huron tried not to laugh as Jake brayed. "That's not nice. Why would someone do that?" he asked.

"The kid was aiming for the lunchroom monitor. She was a really mean lady."

Huron snickered a bit. "Still not nice."

"Ah, who cares? Lighten up," Jake told him. "So where're you from, Aloha?"

Aloha looked down at his feet. "Uh, I was from Rhode Island, but we moved here this summer," he lied.

"Cool," Jake said.

"Yeah, welcome to Siesta Key," Huron added.

"Thanks." Aloha sighed with relief as Jake focused on surfing again.

The rest of the day was spent trying to teach Aloha how to surf while Tails scampered about in the shallow waves near the shore. The sky was beginning to fade into pink and orange hues as the sun went down, and the water was turning a darker shade of blue and getting colder. The boys were all clad in neoprene in preparation for the coldness of dusk's waters.

Though both Aloha and Huron looked tiny on their long surfboards, Jake seemed to be perfectly proportioned on his. The first half hour, Aloha observed Jake and Huron and listened to Jake's instructions. When he felt he had a handle on things, he made his first attempt at surfing. He paddled out on his board and waited for the wave to come. Every time he went to stand up, he made it to his knees. However, because he wasn't used to the way the board shifted underneath him, he slipped off before he could fully stand up. Aloha crashed into the water and sank under the surface, struggling to get back up. Jake watched him come up and gulp in ragged breaths.

"Little dude," Jake said, "you're gonna get used to wiping out. Just be patient and keep at it."

Aloha spat out some water and nodded. They gave up a few hours later. Aloha never managed to get fully upright that first day. But he made some progress the following day. On his fifth attempt, he stood up, a proud grin on his face. His board began to rise in front. He pitched backward as it overbalanced. He leaned to the right to fall sideways into the water and just missed being clocked in the face by the board. When he broke through the surface of the water, he caught his breath and laughed.

"I was up, and then I was down," he joked.

"Oh, man! I thought you were gonna get waffled for sure. Are you all right?" Jake asked.

"I think so."

"What happened?" Huron asked.

"He was too far back," Jake answered.

Aloha shrugged and grinned. It was another hour before he was able to get upright on his surfboard again. This time, though, his feet slipped out from under him, and he went down again.

"What happened that time?" Jake wanted to know.

"I was trying to catch my balance and my feet slipped."

"Yeah, don't try to move your feet forward once you're up. Plant your feet and use your arms to balance you. Also, bend your knees more."

"Okay. I'll try that."

Aloha did better on his next try. The rest of the day, he made it upright but wrestled for control. Jake and Huron were patient. It had taken them weeks to get the hang of it and even longer to master. On the third day, however, Aloha displayed significant improvement. Everything seemed to have clicked for him, and he looked as though he were born to surf. Mari watched as the boy rode up the side of a wave, his knees slightly bent. He used his arms to balance himself as his legs and knees steered the board, much like a skateboarder, and he bent his upper body as he was moving along, synchronizing himself with the roll of the water. He zagged right then lashed left, turning around and going back up over the top of the wave, sliding right down into the barrel. He let the water push him along the wall of the barrel at a slight diagonal. Mari blinked in amazement as he zagged down the tube. The force of the water pushed him out as the barrel collapsed behind him. He veered right again and headed back up the top of the wave. Mari swam alongside him and observed and, from time to time, Aloha would look over with a wonderful smile.

Things were going smoothly for Aloha, which relieved Mari. Yet something was nagging at him. Perhaps it was the way only Aloha could talk to him, or maybe it was the way only Aloha seemed to see him, even though Huron and Jake both looked his way several times. Communicating with him was different when others were around. He used body language to talk to Mari instead of words.

And then there was his swift mastery of surfing. The way he seemed to be part of the waves, not just synchronizing himself with them, made Mari realize that he was born for the sea. Of course, the dolphin had seen surfers before, but Aloha was not just a natural boardhead; he was a son of the sea, riding with even greater grace than Jake and Huron. Noticing this, Mari suspected that Aloha had to be the tide swooner. There was an old legend about a human male also harboring the spirit of the tide. He had previously written it off, because the ocean hadn't seen a tide swooner in centuries. Yet this boy seemed to have the spirit, all right.

According to the legend, the spirit of the sea was bestowed upon one special human being. That human was to use the spirit's powers, sea magic, to protect the oceanic realm from evil things that wished to harm it, since water was a source of life. Mari had known the woman who formerly possessed this spirit. This child, he now realized, had to be her son. When he was born, he must have had part of the spirit passed on to him, staying dormant until the time came when he was to take his mother's place. Oh wow, he's the heir of the maiden, Mari thought, amazed. We've been mourning the same person. This brought a pang of grief to his heart.

Night fell. The water appeared to be black, and the sky was a deep blue with stars crowding the thin clouds. The moon was hovering just above the horizon line, exerting its exotic dance of light on the waves. After another happy day of surfing, the three boys had bonded and experienced the revelation of the waves, as Mari liked to call it. It was a spiritual awakening so fundamental that it literally drew you to it and pulled you in, as the tidal waves pulled the sand from the beach back into the ocean. Aloha followed Jake and Huron home. Their mother had kindly offered to let him stay the night again. Once they put all their surfing gear away, they went up to the deck and had dinner. A couple of hours and a few board games later, they went to bed. Mari stayed to watch the shore, because he really had nowhere else to go.

Aloha the Tide Swooner

Aloha grinned as he lay upon the air mattress beside Huron's bed. He'd had so much fun with Huron and Jake tonight. I like having them as friends, he thought. Plus, it's nice not to have to sleep in the bushes or on the beach. Soon he was asleep with a happy smile still on his face. Inside his dreams, however, was a world filled with horror. He was sitting on a wooden swing in a backyard. The yard sloped down from a hill, and monsters prowled the landscape as he watched. A procession of goblins marched past. They were a little taller than Aloha and reminded him of kids dressed for trick-or-treat. They wore ridiculously colored clothing: purples and reds and outlandish greens, but dread filled him at the thought of what might be lurking at the end of the line. The goblins themselves were not particularly scary looking, but he got an awful feeling as he gazed at them. Their funny costumes contrasted starkly with the repulsive aura that was coming off of them. He shot his gaze up to the sky. Father, help me, he cried as he looked into the sun. So far the goblins had not noticed him, but—

Aloha awoke suddenly. He rubbed his eyes. "Huh? Where am I?" he asked. Then a noise drew his attention. "Mom?" he whispered. His eyes fell on Huron sleeping in his bed. Everything clicked into place. Oh yeah, he thought. The last time I slept indoors was the night before Mom and Dad…He hung his head, angered by the tears coming on. Don't forget your mission, his mom's voice spoke up in his mind. Aloha jumped. His mission. Yes, he had forgotten. He stood up. I gotta get out of here.

The Horato house was swaddled in night, and the sand looked almost as dark as the waves in shadow. There were small valleys of sand basking in the dimness while the moon-kissed hills hoarded all the available light. Ten minutes or so later, Mari saw Aloha walk out the sliding glass door and down the wooden deck stairs onto the beach. He stood on one of the sandy hills. His face was hooded with shade. His eyes drew heavenward.

"Why me, huh? Why did you leave this burden to me?" he yelled.

He fell to his knees, bowing his head as his tears hit the ground, and he crossed his arms over his chest. He began to rock himself back and forth, feeling Mari's eyes upon him. Watching Aloha reminded Mari of how he had felt growing up in the dolphin world without any friends or support. It was as if in his frantic sobs that Aloha was adding Mari's grief to his, for Mari could feel his pain, and he began to wonder if Aloha felt his. The waves picked up in their own frenzy of agony. They slid over Mari, nearly pushing him around as they slammed into him. He saw starfish and sand dollars and a few fish hurled through the air from the fury of the water that was rushing through the shallow depths. He remained immobile as the sea parted around him, hurrying forth to express Aloha's inner turmoil.

Seeing Aloha grieve, Mari flashed back to something that had happened when he was still with his pod. One stormy night, the waters were rioting in the night as the lightning flashed madly. A young dolphin was squealing in fear. Her parents came to her. Mari watched as they nuzzled her. "It's all right. It's just a little lightning. Storms aren't so scary, hon." Taken aback by the memory, Mari wondered, Did my parents ever comfort me like that? He started. Maybe I can be Aloha's comfort, he thought.

As his tears slowed, Aloha lifted his hands toward the sky and stretched his fingers up. "Be still," he commanded. Then his hands collapsed back to his sides, and the sea calmed down a little.

Aloha surveyed the land with a loving gaze. Suddenly, his body lifted up and hovered in the sky. He began to glow as luminescent as the moon. The light he was emitting started pulsating. The water began to get restless again, and the waves rose higher. Aloha looked out at the ocean and stretched out an arm to it as though to halt the breaking waves, which were getting too high for Mari. The waves stopped in midair. Mari gazed at him, mouth open, as Aloha commanded again with humble authority, "Slow."

The waves obeyed. Mari was hypnotized by his teal eyes, perceptive and deep. Those eyes were both youthful and ancient, with a presence of great responsibility. As the Son of the Waves floated above the ground, he looked over at Mari.

"For you, my friend, who continues to watch out for me. Thank you, Mari." His voice boomed but remained in its youthful tone. Mari had expected him to sound older, though he did not know why.

"So you are the tide swooner!" Mari exclaimed.

"I am," he said.

"Then you're the maiden's son, right?"

"Yeah," he replied, "I am." He looked away, wringing his hands.

"What's wrong?" Mari asked.

"Well, it's just, I've known my whole life that I would have this power. My mom"—he hesitated here and got quiet—"was guardian of the ocean. She had these abilities. Her spirit's talent passed to me when she died. I protect the sea now."

"I knew your mother. I went to her funeral right before I met you, Aloha."

Aloha's lower lip quivered, and he teared up again. "I wish I could have been at her and Dad's real funeral." He paused. "I am the last tide swooner, Mari. And it's up to me now to finish the one task my mom didn't accomplish."

"What's that?"

"She was supposed to stop a creature by the name of Barrett. I don't know what he looks like or how to find him, but I know this monster is the ultimate evil. And I am supposed to defeat him somehow. This is the mission she left for me when she died."

Mari gaped. "Not Barrett."

Aloha said, "You know him?"

"I know of him. It is said that he is the source of all evil."

Aloha gulped and nodded.

What a hard task to lay upon his shoulders, Mari thought. It almost seems cruel. "How are you going to find him, Aloha?"

"I don't know. But if it really is my destiny, then I suppose I will find him at some point."

"You're really going to fight him?" Mari asked, astounded.

"I have to. I am who I am," Aloha replied. Odd, he felt very calm all of a sudden.

Something occurred to Mari. "Aloha, when a kid's parents die, and that kid has no family, doesn't the state take the child in or something?

Aloha nodded. "I outwitted them, though. When the paramedics came to help my parents, a crowd was already gathered. I slipped into the bushes during the commotion. I managed to get close to their stretchers for a moment then I ran off. I couldn't let anyone send me to Child Services. How would I accomplish my mission if I was in an orphanage or thrown into foster care?"

"I see." There was a lull in conversation for a moment. Mari changed the subject. "So how do you lift into the air like that? Can you do that all the time?"

He shrugged. "Dunno. There is a lot about this that I don't understand. See, this power, it's not mine. It comes from God. Basically, I'm a conduit for that power. I'm not the source, and I don't have total control over it."

Aloha floated down to earth, said goodnight to Mari, and crept back into the house. Mari frowned. He's the protector of the sea, but he's still a lonely little boy without a family. Who protects him, he wondered. A loyalty so strong that it hurt, welled up inside his heart. All he could do was vow that he would protect the kid.

The next morning, Jake's mom started to make breakfast while the boys sat around the kitchen table. "So what are your plans for today, boys?" she asked.

"I gotta go someplace with my folks," Aloha lied.

"Oh. Well, what are you two doing, Jake, Huron?"

"I'm going to the movies," Jake said.

"And I'm gonna go exploring on Crescent Beach."

"No, dude, you're coming with me. I'm buying."

"Really? Okay."

"Sounds like fun. Well, kids, what would you like for breakfast?"

"Eggs and bacon," Huron said.

"Pancakes and French toast," Jake cried.

"Nothing for me, thanks. I've gotta go," Aloha replied.

Huron looked at him, remembering how he'd passed out when they'd met a few days ago. He narrowed his eyes. "Are you sure you don't want anything?" he asked.

"Nah. Your mom's gone to enough trouble. Besides, we'll probably grab something on the way."

How come his parents let him go that long without eating, Huron asked himself. Noticing Aloha's discomfort, he said, "Okay. See ya."

"Yeah, see ya," Aloha said.

He hurried off before anyone could convince him to stay. He met Mari at their new spot. They played at sea for a few hours before coming back to shore. They reached the beach, when out of nowhere a voice interjected, "Aloha? Are you playing with, with a dolphin?" The duo turned, startled, and there stood Jake and Huron.

Huron looked at Jake and said, "Well of course he is. He's Mr. Mystery, can't you see? Who's your friend, Aloha?"

Jake looked back and forth from Mari to Aloha.

"His name's Mari, Huron," Aloha answered, beaming with pride. They had discovered the secret. What does this mean for us, Mari wondered.

"Cool."

"Dude, that's wicked awesome," Jake exclaimed. Huron rolled his eyes at Jake. Jake shoved him playfully, and they both started laughing. From behind them came a very soft *woof*. Aloha smiled as his new friends turned to see Tails wagging his tail behind them and gazing at them with pleading eyes.

Jake said, "We couldn't forget you, Tails."

Tails ran to him, jump-hugged him, and licked his face. Aloha cracked up, and Huron said, "Ooh, looks like Jake's got a new girlfriend!"

Both boys looked at one another as Jake turned red and laughed. He smirked, grabbed Huron, and gave him a noogie. Aloha ran to shore and hugged the dog, who besieged him with dog kisses. Huron and Jake joined in the hug, and Mari longed to be part of it. He rethought that as all of them rushed into the water and threw their arms about him, crowding him and chaffing his slick skin. Tails began licking him and barking.

Aloha and Mari soon resumed their schedule, incorporating Jake and Huron into it as well. They decided from now on to plan water events so that Mari could be part of their fun. Jake also agreed to take them boating so that Tails could go. Mari had thought it would be hard sharing Aloha with them, but it wasn't because they shared themselves with him, too. Despite Jake, Huron, and Tails becoming part of the gang, Mari caught on that Aloha wanted to keep their communication a secret, because he hadn't told them about it.

When the others left for the day, Mari said, "You ever been to Eden, sailor?"

"Eden? No, where's that?"

"About a half mile from here. It's an unpopulated area filled with lots of natural vegetation. You'd love it."

"Show me."

"I'll tell you how to get there then meet you there. Tricky navigation, but I've done it before."

"How come you never showed me before?" Aloha asked.

"Because getting there from the ocean is life-threatening for a human and very difficult, to say the least, for a dolphin. And also, I forgot."

"Why is it so dangerous?"

"Sharp currents, jagged rocks, and a whirlpool underneath the surface. Trust me, aside from preservation acts, that's the thing that's kept humans away from there. A couple of kids nearly lost their lives swimming in that small inlet beyond the bridge."

"Wow. So how do you get there then?"

"From land, you have to walk to the southern tip of Turtle Beach, and there you will see a grassy hill with a boulder sitting next to it. In front of these landmarks is a rope bridge that extends across the water to a small island. That's Eden. Be careful on the bridge. It's old and slick, and the jagged rocks I was talking about before are jutting up underneath and around the bridge. You wouldn't want to fall on those."

"Yikes. Still, sounds cool. See ya there."

"Right."

It was a ten-minute walk for Aloha. He passed through some wildly unkempt plants and grasses at the southern point of the beach and finally saw the hill and the large stone. Each had a wooden pole in front of it. Hooked to the poles were the supports of the bridge. Aloha beheld the rickety rope bridge with cautious eyes. He swallowed hard and placed a hand on one frayed rope rail. As he did so, the planks creaked and the bridge lurched sideways a bit. All I did was touch it, he thought. His breath came out in shallow huffs. He hesitated, his other hand gripping one of the wooden posts. I guess it's now or never. His throat constricted for a moment as he stepped onto the ancient-looking boards. He waited a few seconds to be sure the bridge wasn't going to move uncontrollably or collapse on him. The boards held his weight. He proceeded across. Although the bridge was never entirely stable and was in constant, yet moderate motion, Aloha became oblivious to this as he focused on the island looming before him.

It was like a pirate's fantasy: clandestine and beckoning, teeming with primitive growth. There were large rocks strewn about the small beach. Beyond that was a tropical forest of potential adventure among the brush and ferns and overhanging palm fronds. Aloha was amazed at the lush vegetation in spite of the rugged terrain. He saw Mari waiting for him from a safe distance.

"It's beautiful!" he exclaimed.

"Now you know why they call it Eden, sailor."

"Mari, we should hang out here."

"You can hang here with Jake and Huron, but the deathtrap entrance and exit is not for me."

He nodded. They headed back to Turtle Beach, and Aloha took a nap in the sand while Mari swam around. That night the two went fishing. The idea had come to Mari after he had seen Aloha pass out on the beach. When Aloha had returned the following morning from Huron's, Mari brought up his idea. Aloha had reluctantly agreed, and they'd been doing it ever since. It remained awkward trying to catch the fish without the proper equipment. He had to catch them barehanded or rely on Mari to grab them in his jaws. Aloha still grimaced as he killed the fish and ate them raw. He always gagged after he got the first few bites down, then dry heaved for a moment. But in the end, he usually managed to keep it down. After they ate, Mari spoke.

"Aloha, shouldn't you tell everyone who you are?"

He shook his head. "Mom said that a good leader doesn't need to declare his or her self. Instead, I should prove who I am by my actions. That's what she did."

"Oh."

Aloha hadn't seen Jake and Huron in two days. He was on his way to meet Mari when the sounds of laughter and shouting drew his attention. There were Jake and Huron and their parents relaxing on the beach. They were playfully shoving each other and chasing each other around, just as he and his parents used to do. His heart hammered in his chest. His face turned red. A gurgling sound arose in his throat as the breath was knocked out of him. He slunk away, angered by the sight. Huron glanced up, sensing his movement. Why didn't he come over, he wondered.

"Mom, can Jake and I be excused?" Huron asked.

"All right, but don't be gone too long. We're having lunch soon."

"Okay."

Huron grabbed his puzzled brother and tugged him along. When they were out of their parents' earshot, Jake said, "What's going on?"

"I just saw Aloha. He looked really upset. Let's follow him and see what's up."

"Okay," Jake replied.

It was a bright morning, the sky was a pale blue, and Mari was waiting for Aloha to show up. He saw the kid in the distance. He grew happy until he noticed how Aloha was stomping his way down the beach. His hands were balled into fists, and his shoulders sagged. He tromped through the water, making such a racket that Mari cringed. Aloha shoved his fists into his pockets.

"What's wrong?" Mari asked.

"Nothing."

"Come on, I can tell you're upset."

"I feel so alone. I'm the only person left alive in my family. Why? What's the point of that?"

"I don't know, but one day it will make sense. Trust that there is a purpose for what has happened."

"But it's so hard sometimes. I don't think I can do it."

"You have to. It's just the way life is."

"I know."

"Besides, you're not alone. You have me."

"I know, but look at Huron and Jake. I get so jealous because they have each other, and I have no one."

"Aloha, see, we're brothers of a kind, you and me. We both have a kinship with the sea."

"You're right, but Jake and Huron are real brothers," he cried.

"If this friendship isn't a form of brotherhood, then what is it?" Mari asked.

"It is," he confirmed, "but they have…oh, I don't know."

"Parents?"

"Yeah," he whispered. His eyes widened alertly. "Huh? He's here!" he suddenly murmured. He turned his head and looked over his right shoulder. Mari didn't see anything. Aloha began to cry again. "Oh, Mari," he said, "he was there. He was right here. I felt him."

"Who was?"

"My dad. Or his spirit was, anyway. He's still with me." Aloha smiled. "He's still with me, in here, inside."

"Where at?" Mari asked, baffled.

"In my memories. Where my mom is, too."

As Aloha said this, there appeared the man who had held the beach towel. He had his hand on Aloha's shoulder, but he was gazing at Mari. His eyes were sad. Before Mari could look closer, the man was gone again. He was starting to think fate was playing some kind of game with him. This spirit, Aloha's father, had stared at him like he was supposed to do something about the fact that his son was feeling so horribly alone. Figures, he thought. Even my best friend's parental spirit disapproves of me, just like all the dolphin parents did. What am I, the bane of parental existence?

"Oh," Mari replied. He was glad this realization had brought Aloha happiness. Maybe his parents were somewhere inside, too. But then again, Mari couldn't remember them like Aloha could his. A voice interrupted them.

"You're an orphan," came Huron's voice. Aloha froze.

"You can talk to dolphins?" asked Jake.

Aloha nodded the affirmative to both questions. He looked down at the ground, shuffling his feet. Huron and Jake could see that he didn't want to talk about it.

"I think it's awesome that you can talk to dolphins," Huron told him, changing the subject.

"Thanks," Aloha mumbled.

"Yeah, but Huron can turn into a wolf," bragged Jake.

"Jake," Huron snapped. Aloha and Mari were bug-eyed.

"Aw, come on, Huron, show them."

Now Huron looked uncomfortable and shook his head. Jake whispered, "He and Tails can talk to each other, too."

"Wow," Aloha exclaimed. "I didn't know that was possible."

"But you can talk to dolphins. Is it really that big of a stretch that I can talk to Tails?" Huron asked.

"I guess not, but I can't transform into an animal, either. I don't know if I believe that's even possible."

"C'mon, bro, end the controversy. Show him your wolf form," Jake cajoled.

"Oh, all right."

Huron tilted his head back and howled. He really sounds like a wolf, Aloha thought. As he howled, a bright, yellow-gold light surrounded him, radiating outward from his chest. Suddenly he flipped into the air and emerged as a wolf. His body was gray with white on his paws and muzzle. He still had his purple hair and pink eyes. Aloha gawked, backing up.

"Don't be afraid," Wolf-Huron said.

"You can talk too?"

"Yes."

"How are you able to do that?"

"Tails came to me one day in the forest back in Minnesota. He showed me I could do this. He said it was a gift from God to help me with the bullies." Huron smiled shyly.

"I see," Aloha croaked.

Jake tapped Huron's forehead. "Bro, you better change again. We have to get back. Mom'll be mad if we're late for lunch."

"Oh yeah," Huron replied. He stood very still with his eyes closed. He appeared to be deep in thought. At last, a white light formed around him and eclipsed him. As he grew taller, the light stretched upward. The light faded and there was human Huron standing there.

"We'll see you later," Jake told Aloha.

"Bye," Aloha said with a wave.

When they were gone, Mari said, "I didn't know there were other people with different powers. Did you?"

"No. It's weird. I thought mom's family were the only ones with supernatural abilities," Aloha said, wrinkling his forehead.

"Your dad didn't have any powers?" Mari asked.

Aloha shook his head. "Nope. It was passed down through my mom's side."

"How do you know you're the last tide swooner, then?"

Aloha's eyes widened. "Well, I assume that I am, since it's my job to stop Barrett."

"I see. Once he's gone, evil will be gone. I guess there wouldn't need to be another one, then, huh?"

"Nope," Aloha confirmed.

Later that day, Jake and Huron came back, this time with Tails. Huron suggested they go boating.

"What do ya say, Aloha, bro?" Jake asked.

"Yeah," Aloha cried.

Tails barked in agreement. Jake drove the boat out about a half a mile from the shore. Mari swam beside them as Tails, ever present, kept pace above him, his tongue lolling in a playful manner. Aloha talked to Mari about plans that were being made with the others for tomorrow, and when he got sick of translating Mari's side of the conversation, he touched his hands to both his friends' mouths and said, "Dolphin speak." Nothing happened.

"What'd you do that for, Aloha?" Jake asked.

"Yeah, you kinda freaked me out with that whole touching our mouths thing," Huron added.

"You'll see," Aloha said. Both kids looked disappointed.

Mari gazed up at them curiously. "What did you do?" the dolphin asked. Jake and Huron's jaws dropped as their eyes grew large.

"Whoa. This is great. I can understand him," Huron said exuberantly.

"Me too," Jake exclaimed.

"Hey, how did you do that?" Huron asked.

"He has powerful gifts. He's the tide swooner, guardian and Son of the Waves," Mari explained.

"Oh," Jake and Huron said in unison.

Children never failed to amaze Mari. In most cases, they asked more questions than adults did, but in all the situations adults would question, they had unfailing faith and belief. He often wondered how and why that changed in these creatures. Where along the way did they lose their imagination, belief, and wonder? From that day on, they all spoke the same language. As the three boys walked to the beach house that evening to see if Aloha could spend the night again, Huron whispered to Jake, "What are we gonna do about Aloha?"

"I don't know," Jake responded, perturbed.

Aloha heard this and said, "I'm not your problem. Forget about it."

"Hey, Aloha?"

"Yeah, Huron?"

"How did your parents die?"

"A car accident, couple of days before I met you."

"Whoa, harsh," Jake replied.

"I'll say," Aloha muttered.

"Dude, I got an idea. You could sleep at our house, like, permanently, and all you gotta do is be careful not to run into our parents."

"Jake, that's not going to work. They'd find him in our house."

"Nah, bro, see, he can sleep *at* our house, not *in* our house. Here's what we'll do," he said and began to whisper.

For a week, they let Aloha, with his trusty backpack as a pillow, sleep underneath the deck so their parents wouldn't see and fed him. Jake did his laundry for him and told him when his parents weren't home so that he could shower. Aloha was grateful for their kindness, even if it seemed somewhat bizarre. Eventually, their parents caught on (mostly from the depleted food supply in the fridge) and found out what they were doing.

Huron and Jake were sitting at the kitchen table that night after their parents had supposedly gone up to bed. They were thinking about Aloha all alone outside under the deck, when they heard footsteps coming down the stairs. A moment later, their mother came into the kitchen. She smiled at them as she reached for the handle of the refrigerator. Neither of them thought about it. She opened the door, her face full of astonishment. Uh-oh, Huron and Jake thought.

"Boys," she said, turning to them. "Didn't I just get groceries last week? What happened? Did you both decide to have growth spurts and not tell me?"

"Uh, well, Mom, it's just, we, uh," Jake trailed off.

"Uh-huh. I'm waiting. Tell me where all the food has gone." She drummed her fingers on the countertop for emphasis.

"Okay, see, it's not like we adopted a kid or something."

"Jake," Huron yelled.

"Are you guys hiding another dog or something from us that is consuming our groceries?" she asked suspiciously.

"No, see Aloha was here, and he's been here a lot," Jake stammered.

"I knew it," she said.

"Huh?" they asked.

"I knew there was something odd about him when we met him. I love him, and so does your father. See, he's never had us meet his parents, and you guys have never gone to his house, so it's just a guess, but is he homeless?"

Huron decided to let Jake handle Mom. Jake was good at explaining things that he had trouble with.

"Okay, okay. You caught us. See, Aloha's parents died in a car accident two days before we met. Huron found him on the beach, passed out from hunger. Huron shared his lunch with him and brought him home to spend the night. We found out about his parents by accident. They were all he had. So we decided to have him sleep under the deck and help him out."

She shook her head. "I cannot believe this, you two. Jake, how could you let him sleep under there? Do we not have a basement?"

"Uh, yeah, Mom."

"Huron, how could you let him come up with this bizarre idea and actually carry it out? Why didn't you just tell us? Oh, boys, what will I do with you? Okay, is he out there right now?"

"Yeah."

"We'll take care of him, then. It's settled. Jimmy! Get down here," she shouted at the stairs.

He came bounding down the stairs. "Yes, sweetheart?"

"Do you care for the boys' friend, Aloha?"

"Yeah, he's all right." He narrowed his eyes. "Why?"

"Because our boys have been letting him sleep underneath the deck with sand bugs and who knows what else and feeding him because he's an orphan. What do you say we officially make him part of this family?"

"I think that's an excellent idea, Marisol. Wait, is he still under the deck?"

"Yes."

"Let's go," he said, adding, "I'm guessing that this was Jake's idea. Huron, how could you let him do that?"

"Sorry, Dad." Huron blushed

"Hey," Jake said.

They walked onto the deck and down the steps. Marisol leaned down and smiled at the wide-eyed Aloha, who had heard them coming. "Hello, Aloha."

"Hi, Mrs. Horato."

"Come with us, please, son," Jimmy told him.

He did as they asked, nervous. They led him into the kitchen.

"Have a seat." Aloha sat down.

"Now, Aloha, if you're going to be our son, you're going to need to know that this kitchen is where all serious family discussions and meetings are held. Okay, son?"

"Okay—huh? You want to, to adopt me?" he asked, surprised and delighted.

"Yes, we do. We'll go talk to the attorney and the Child Services people tomorrow."

"But what if they take me away to some institution or a foster home?"

"Well, they might, but we think we have a pretty good chance. You see, we figured out pretty quickly what was probably going on with you, so we've already talked to them. All they want to know is your history and some information. Then, if everything is in order, we can go to court, and the attorney will ask you if you want to be adopted, and if you say yes—"

"If?" Aloha interrupted, incredulous.

Marisol smiled and continued, "Then they will take us into the courtroom, and the attorney will tell them that you wish to have us adopt you, and then we will become your legal guardians."

The Sword

Two Years Later

Mari watched the man of wars swim by, shimmering in the narrow beams of sunlight reaching the water. Because he was in shallow water, his tail grazed a few brittle stars who survived but had some rather huffy words for him. He dove under the water, watching some chitons scatter from the rocks below. A couple of stingrays passed him, and then a small octopus thrust its way up for a moment, saw Mari, and squirted ink at him as though he were its fiercest predator. Riled, Mari hurried back to the surface. It wasn't nice, but he hoped the octopus' tentacles got caught in some seaweed. That was cruel enough, but he had once seen a squid run beak-first into a coral reef.

Though there were heavy clouds hanging in the sky that day, it was balmy out, and the sea was reflecting the gray of the clouds. The clouds looked innocent enough, no hint of an oncoming storm. Behind him was a dock, and in front of him was a pile of sand and rocks extending out from the shore. And on that pile of rocks stood a boy. Mari looked over at him, and a chill slithered its way down his vertebrae. Tension throbbed in the air. A waft of negative energy assaulted his face. It felt as if he'd been smacked.

The kid had an odd appearance. His blond hair was a pale, unnatural shade of yellow, like the color of watered down lemonade. Mari could easily believe the boy had drawn the clouds above to him to shroud himself from the sun. Unlike Aloha, the stranger did not radiate any sense of vitality. Nothing about him hinted at the sort of vulnerability and innocence that kids possess. His deadly calm and composed manner evoked coldness in Mari's soul. Perhaps it was his eyes, which were a fierce and faded blue that reminded him of death. His pupils were not black but a light gray color that made him seem even more imposing. As he glance Mari's way, the dolphin saw his expression turn into a scowl of black hatred.

The boy turned and stalked off over the rock pile. Mari remained still for quite some time, transfixed by this preternatural meeting. As he began to stir, he suddenly realized what was the most peculiar about this stranger. He had been wearing a long-sleeved navy blue uniform shirt with a high collar and six metal buttons down the front, and a pair of brown slacks and black leather shoes. For anyone dealing with the Florida summer, this attire would be considered abnormal, but for a kid, this outfit seemed inappropriate, a little sinister, even. Where would you get a shirt like that for a child, he wondered. He was scanning the shore for Aloha when he had an epiphany. Those eyes, Mari thought. He had gotten a chill from looking in that boy's eyes, and it clicked now that his eyes hadn't seemed alive. They were the eyes of a corpse: pale and floating and lifeless. Mari shivered and continued on toward shore.

"Mari," came the excited half-shout, half-laugh of his good friend. Instantly, he felt warmed by happiness, all trace of unease subsiding. Aloha's eyes were bright with joy.

"Aloha. Where ya been, sailor?"

Aloha was running at breakneck speed along the shore, legs stretching out as his arms propelled him forward. Mari lifted up one fin and waved as Aloha scrambled along the dock in his usual fashion. He swam over.

"Shall we go exploring?" Aloha asked.

"Absolutely," he agreed.

They swam out into that beautiful green Gulf of Mexico filled with exuberance. Along the way, they played a game of water tag, dodging about and tagging, sometimes hiding behind buoys and other obstacles in the water or going under and trying to catch each other.

"I wish Jake and Huron were here. This game would be a lot more fun."

"Yeah, you're right. Maybe we should have ourselves a treasure hunt, sailor. What do you say?"

"Ar. Let's do it."

"All righty, sailor."

He dove and began turning his head to and fro in a frenzied search for booty. Mari imitated him from below. Aloha's arms and legs moved in awkward motions. It was as if he was trying to imitate a frog. He wasn't doing very well at it, but he kept on. As Mari observed, he marveled at the usefulness of legs. Aloha could walk on land, swim, and kick things. Fins didn't allow such conveniences. Although satisfied with his limitations most of the time, every so often he found himself living the life that wasn't possible for him through Aloha. He finished this brief reflection on limitations and ran smack into the hull of a sunken ship. His head glanced off the side, but his snout missed the impact, thank goodness.

"Mari, you did it. You found a sh—are you all right?" Aloha garbled, having to surface directly after he got these words out; he forgot that he could not breathe underneath the water, nor could he speak well, though Mari understood him just fine. Once he caught his breath on the surface, he swam back down to his friend.

Mari groaned and gave a small nod when he returned. His head was reeling. Aloha frowned and put one soft—and cold—little hand on Mari's aching head and gave him a massage. Back and forth, his hand moved. Mari blinked as he felt a tingling sensation replacing the pain. He smiled with gratitude. Aloha shrugged in reply. After his run-in with the ship, he grew excited, completely engaged in their game. Aloha looked down and signaled to him to surface so they could discuss how to go about exploring the ship. Mari zoomed upward in a delightful race with him and whipped him good. Aloha threw his arms around Mari's neck with glee.

"Mari, you're the best. I can't believe you found an actual sunken ship."

"What if we don't find any treasure?" he asked, his eagerness starting to fade. What if there are human remains on it, he thought, the skin between his pectorals beginning to shrivel a bit.

"Don't you know," Aloha said, "that the treasure is in the adventure?"

"Oh, so it doesn't matter if we find anything?" If Mari could have scratched his head, he would have.

"We've already found something, silly."

Humans. They were so confounding sometimes. And yet, he had to admit that Aloha was right. His statement had been both enigmatic and simple at the same time, as though it had layers of meaning far beyond what he realized at the moment. Mari gazed down as he followed Aloha into the bowels of the rotted wooden ship, which was about twenty meters long and seven meters wide, and realized that there was nothing but sand on the nearby sea bottom. What an extremely dull place to end up. You'd think if there was any dignity in defeat that the ship would have at least landed in an exciting and scenic place, he thought. They began a brief exploration of the deck. It wasn't easy to do, because the ship had sunken on its side, so the deck was canted at an awkward, precarious angle. The dolphin made slow rounds around the mildewed tomb. Aloha was swimming around on the top deck, grabbing the capsized mast to keep from sinking.

There wasn't much to see in the wreckage of the broken bow or the cargo hold except abandoned chasms of gloom, but journeying through the darkness together made it very satisfying. It was like being in a haunted house with your best friend and daring something to happen. There was no treasure, but being inside that tunnel of wood with such a fearless creature was enough. Except for a rusty dagger, there was little to excite the imagination. Aloha picked up the dagger and stuck the sheathed blade in his pocket. Mari gestured, waving his pectorals around in half circles, that this was not a good idea, that he could cut himself, but Aloha shook his head. Once he had the dagger snug in his pocket, he grabbed Mari's dorsal and pointed up. Mari took him to the surface, where he gasped for breath.

"Why didn't you tell me to come up sooner, sailor?"

"I saw the dagger, and I wanted to get it."

Mari rolled his eyes. "You know, we could have gone back to retrieve it."

He shook his head again. "No. That would have taken too long. Besides, I would have forgotten where it was, anyway."

"Wait a minute. How in the world did you hold your breath that long? And how did you manage to swim that deep without scuba gear?"

"Must be some kind of magic, I guess," he teased. "No, seriously, it forms a sort of protective bubble around my face, kinda like a space helmet."

"I don't get it, Aloha. Why did you gag for breath if you can use your power to do that stuff?"

"Well, there are limitations," he stated simply, leaving his friend in frustrated suspense.

"Okay, so what are the limitations?"

"Hmmm, don't know. Guess I've got a lot of learning to do, huh?"

"So why didn't you do that the first time then?"

"Because I was still trying to figure out how to do it. My mom used to be able to do this, but she never showed me how."

"Didn't your mom teach you anything?"

He grew silent for a moment. "She taught me wisdom, not how to use this power. She trusted in me to be able to learn on my own, I guess."

"I get it. So how does it work, anyway?"

"I suck the oxygen atoms out of the water molecules. It's kinda like slurping it in. But I still have to learn how to sustain it," Aloha responded.

"Oh. So, what do you think happened to that ship?"

He shrugged. "Maybe some pirates attacked it." His eyes glinted with excitement.

"Nah, I think maybe it was a bad design."

He gave the dolphin a funny look.

"What?" Mari protested. "It could happen."

Aloha paused. "Why here? I mean, this location isn't exactly ideal for that kind of nautical travel."

"It doesn't really make sense. I guess that's a mystery we'll never know the answer to."

"Sure we will. We'll just ask God when we get to heaven."

Mari snickered at his answer and said, "Okay. Do you want to go back down?" He certainly didn't want to. That prison hole down there creeped him out. It was a grinning skeleton trapped in a watery ship's cemetery.

"Nah. Let's go back to shore. I'm hungry." Aloha put his arms around Mari's neck so that he could carry him.

"Okey dokey, sailor. You know the drill."

He nodded, and Mari swam them back to shore so he could go home to eat lunch. While Aloha was gone, he watched the seagulls and pelicans fly swiftly across the sky. He began to imagine what it would feel like to be able to skate along those clouds and get closer to the sun, free of the restraints of the earth. His thoughts rattled on in various tangents. Mari's gaze meandered from the sky to the nearby boat docks. He started when he noticed the kid from earlier observing him from the pier. His stare gave off the black, slithery aura of evil. Hours seemed to pass as they locked eyes. Mari decided to test out a theory he had. He swam left and right in zigzag motions, his eyes on the stranger all the while. The stranger's glower followed his every movement. Now that Mari knew for sure that this glare was directed at him, he swam toward the kid. The boy's jack-o-lantern smirk spread slowly across his face until his mouth settled into a wicked smile.

"Enjoy it while it lasts," he told the dolphin in a gruff, resounding voice, startling Mari half out of his wits. "Your time is coming, guardian." Then he laughed the bitter, haunting laugh of an evil genius.

"What the dickens?" Mari said.

He turned with a menacing grimace and disappeared—literally—into thin air. Why come after me, Mari thought. I'm nothing special. The next thing he knew, the hues of dusk had come upon the world. Whatever that creature was, he was of small stature like a child, but his eyes were not childlike. There was absolutely no humanity in those eyes. Mari suspected he was one of the great legendary evils, although he reasoned that he didn't even know whether or not the legends he had been told were even true. Sure, the one about Aloha had been true, but what were the odds that all of them were true? And what did he mean when he called Mari *guardian*? I don't remember any legend about a guardian, he thought. When at last Aloha returned, Mari could not focus on anything. He was much too afraid of the diabolical possibilities that the stranger held.

"Mari, are you all right?"

"Huh? Yeah," he replied, distracted.

Aloha narrowed his eyes suspiciously. "It's dark. I can't stay. You take care, all right?"

Mari replied with a nod. Aloha went home, glancing numerous times over his shoulder at him with a fretted countenance. Mari shrugged it off as he swam away, alone once more.

That evening both of them had what seemed like a terrible nightmare. It started with Mari realizing that he was underwater and couldn't breathe. They were about twenty yards from shore. Aloha was watching from a spot just above Mari, where he was floating in the air. An enormous, abysmal shadow fell over them. There was a form in the blackness, but neither could see what it was. When it spoke, Mari thought he vaguely recognized the voice.

He was magnetized by the hideous voice as it repeated, "Sleep. Sleep." The voice mesmerized the dolphin into a state of unconsciousness. His eyes shut. His body began to sink.

What do I do, Aloha thought. The voice had almost hypnotized him, but the cold sprays of sea water in his face woke him again. Mari's underwater, and he can't surface for air! Aloha lifted his hands and gestured wildly as he screamed at the offending voice to stop. His voice was raw with fear. Maybe he could use his power to make the sea hurl Mari out. I might be able to suspend him in the air, he thought, except I don't even know how I'm able to do it. When he tried to get the sea to extract Mari by thrusting his arms outward and upward as he had when he calmed the sea, nothing happened. I'm too weak, he realized. He tried again. The best he could do was to stop Mari's body from sinking farther, but he could not lift Mari up to the surface. Desperate, he cried out.

"Mari," he shouted, "Wake up!"

Mari's eyelids fluttered. Aloha shrieked at him again. This time, he snapped awake and managed to get to the surface just in time. The shrouded figure, frustrated at being thwarted, said to Aloha, "You're next, tide swooner."

Out of nowhere, Mari yelled, "The sword! You must use the sword!"

"Silence," demanded that awful voice. The sky flashed white then turned dark red. But the awful red faded swiftly, revealing the regular night sky.

Without warning, the voice and the figure were gone. Mari looked up at the sky to see Aloha with a golden glow radiating about him as he began to float back to shore. He saw Aloha's eyes close, his body still shivering from the ocean spray, for he was very low in the air and kept getting hit by the backsplash of the waves. His clothes were soaked, and his hair was full of glittering sea salt.

Mari's dream morphed into another one. There he was in a parking lot. He barely made out the yellow-orange parking dividers because everything was fuzzy and unclear. The atmosphere was a very bright yellow, which contrasted with the light gray of the asphalt. It was clear that this was supposed to be a sky and parking lot, but it looked somewhat like an impressionist painting. He looked around and saw the blurred outline of a little boy with black hair. He squinted in an effort to make out more detail. It was no use. All he could see was the blurry boy watching two tall silhouettes walk away. Mari held out a fin to him, but the scene cleared. He awoke from the dream then, having no idea how he'd gotten where he was. His throat was hoarse. He was short of breath. He looked up to the sky, and his heart slammed against his ribs. A slumbering Aloha floated through the air, surrounded by a brilliant golden light. The light circulated outward from his body as he sailed home, completely unaware of what was going on.

The next morning, Aloha came up to him with a confused look on his face. "Mari, I had this weird dream last night."

"So did I; tell me about it."

"Was yours about an evil presence and a sword or something? Were you unconscious in the dream?"

"Yeah."

"That was my dream, too. Only, I'm not sure if it was a dream. This morning when I woke up, my clothes were soaked with sea water, and my hair and skin were encrusted with salt."

"You think all that really happened?" Mari asked.

"I don't know."

"When I woke up, I saw you floating through the air, glowing with gold."

Aloha gasped. "So it did happen!"

"I think it did."

"Weird. What do you think it means?"

"I don't know. Hey, did you have another short dream after that one?" Mari inquired.

Aloha crinkled his nose. "What do you mean?"

"Never mind. I can barely remember it, anyway."

"You sure it's not important?"

"Yeah."

Thinking about their dreams reminded Mari of the boy he had met in the harbor the day before. He refused to tell Aloha about the kid with the zombie-like corpse eyes. There was no use in scaring him. After a few more hours, Mari had successfully shoved down all his worries about the menacing boy and the dream, but it all came rushing back full force while Aloha was walking along the beach collecting shells. All of a sudden, he positively squeaked with delight. He bent down and picked up something red. It had a hilt sticking out of it, and Mari realized that it was a sword. A feeling of dread permeated his mind. What if he hurts himself, he wondered, envisioning all the things that could happen. Even as he was thinking about it, he noticed the red case. It was made of some sturdy leathery material instead of wood or metal. The adventurous boy unsheathed the maroon-gripped sword and swung it around as though it were made expressly for him. Mari heard himself screaming in his head, "The sword! You must use the sword!" He again pictured the evil boy from the docks. The questing sound of the waves snapped him out of the flashback.

They lapped gently in their slow, constant motion. It sounded like a hand tapping against someone's forearm. To him, the waves seemed to be forever rolling over the world around them, pushing forward. They were the one thing he knew of in life that didn't have at least some small fear of moving forward. They didn't hesitate or hold back.

Aloha called to him, jerking him out of his reverie. "Mari. You see this?"

"Yes. I see it. But maybe you better put that thing down. You could hurt yourself."

"Nah. I'll be careful."

Mari watched him play with the sword. That weird dream or whatever it was weighed on his mind, nagging him. How could he even have a dream? It was impossible. Dolphins can't dream, he thought. Mari was scared, and he noted with envy that Aloha was laughing and swiping the air with his new present.

With graceful motions, he battled with unseen foes, growling out every now and then or shouting, "You'll never win, you cursed heal."

Aloha fell to his knees without warning, breathing hard. He sprawled out onto his stomach, stirring great alarm in his dolphin companion. Then he said with deep conviction and determination, "This isn't over. I won't be down for long." That said and an imaginary fire in his eyes, he picked himself up off of the ground and shot forward, swashbuckling with someone only he could see. His playtime went on in this fashion for an hour. Eventually, Jake came to get him for dinner. He and Huron had just gotten back from skateboarding, something that they enjoyed but Aloha didn't. He wasn't very good at it.

"Aloha." Jake greeted him with a wave.

"Hey," Aloha replied in a distant voice, utterly absorbed.

"Where'd you get that?" Jake asked, meaning the sword.

"Found it."

"Oh. I see. Finders keepers, losers weepers, eh?"

"Yeah."

"All right, cool. Time for dinner, man. So where are you gonna keep that thing? You can't show it to Mom. She'd freak."

Aloha smiled. "I'll bury it in the sand under the deck."

"Dude, if Mom can find you under there, then I think she can probably find a sword."

"She hasn't found the crowbar I hid under there that I found along the road or the dagger I found with Mari."

"You have a crowbar and a dagger hidden under our deck? Wicked! Dad'd have a coronary."

"Tell me about it," Aloha responded, rolling his eyes.

"Just promise me one thing."

"What's that?"

"That you won't end up stashing cereal under there. I mean, you know, it would kind of sorta bring disgrace to our family."

Aloha grinned at him and said, "You are weird. Okay, I solemnly swear never to bring shame to our family by desecrating cereal boxes or the contents, or at least I'll leave the Cheerios and the Frosted Flakes. But if it comes down to Lucky Charms, I can't promise anything. Those marshmallows are just too tasty."

"You can take me Cheerios, but you'll ne'er get me Lucky Charms."

"You can keep your Lucky Charms as long as I can have me pot o' gold. A leprechaun has ta have sumthin' y'know," Aloha replied with a fake Irish accent.

Jake cracked up and clapped his hand on his little brother's shoulder, saying, "Bro, you know, I love you!" He waved to Mari as they left. "Toodles, Mari."

"Check ya later," Mari told him.

Shakoda the Summoner

"Jake, you cannot." Huron glowered at him.

"Yes, you can."

"For the last time, you cannot. Once you're dead, that's it."

"Dude, haven't you ever read *Frankenstein?* And you call yourself smart."

Huron slapped his forehead then rubbed it to get rid of the pain. "Jake, that is a work of fiction. There is no way that the dead can be fully reanimated. And there is definitely no way they could think, even if it were possible, which it's not."

"But what about the one dude who did the experiment with electric current? He got a body to move."

"You can reanimate a corpse with electricity, but that doesn't make it alive. You can't bring someone's soul back from heaven. Ergo, a reanimated corpse cannot think. And there is still no way to get the body fully reanimated. That's just not possible."

"What about zombies?"

"Zombies are not real."

"Prove it."

"You're some kind of weirdo, you know that?"

"No, you just don't have any imagination."

"Even if zombies were real, they are incapable of thought, thus corroborating my point."

"Yeah? Well, you just better watch out, or Frankenstein will eat you one of these days."

Huron glared at him. "Um, imbecile, Frankenstein is the name of the creature's creator. The creature never had a name."

"Oh lay off, ya killjoy."

"Guys, can we just get going?" Aloha interjected.

"Sure," Jake said as he loaded their gear into the boat.

The three of them were going fishing. Tails also accompanied them. He and Huron sat on one end of the boat making faces at each other as they talked. As for Mari, he was busy planning mischief. He waited about an hour before putting his plan into action. Mari quickly bit down—carefully, so as not to hurt himself—on Huron's line. He jerked it lightly, making sure to keep clear of the hook so it didn't cinch itself between his teeth, then he clamped down and pulled hard. Huron came tumbling into the water with a dazed expression. As he was dunked beneath the waves, his eyes shifted about in search of the cause of his being dragged overboard. When he noticed Mari, his mouth widened in surprise.

As Mari returned his stare, his surprise melted away. Huron's uniquely colored eyes filled with delectation. Above them, Tails looked into the green water, unconcerned. Huron grabbed Mari's dorsal. Mari took the hint and swam far away from the boat, where they surfaced. Pockets of sunshine doused Huron, making shadows under the water droplets sliding down his face.

"Mari, that was great. You stinker." He uttered a contented sigh.

"Hey, let's play a joke on them."

"What'll we do?" Huron asked.

"We'll sneak back to the boat underwater so they don't see us. They'll be in for a surprise, don't you think?"

"Yeah!"

Mari told him to hold his breath, and down they went. Mari sped to the boat, and they surfaced at the back where no one could see.

"Huron!" Jake was shouting, about ready to jump in after him.

"Mari will protect him, if he isn't the cause of this." Aloha had a guilty smile on his face.

Jake relaxed a bit. Huron and Mari slowly made their way to the side of the boat. Tails barked happily. Jake turned their way and looked at them, his unease dissolving. Huron burst out laughing.

Now it was Aloha's turn to play mother hen. "Huron, are you all right?"

"Yeah. Mari, you're all right, you are, old chap," Huron informed him as he caught his breath. Jake helped him back up into the boat.

Aloha gave Mari a joking lecture, with Jake making mock threats every time he paused. Jake stared hard at Huron, who could not stop smiling. Rolling his eyes, Jake turned and stomped off to the other side of the boat. Aloha turned to Huron, who shrugged. Huron hurried over to Jake, who shouted, "That was not funny. You hear me? Not funny. Don't ever do that again. I mean it."

Taken aback, Huron said, "I'm sorry, okay? I won't do it again."

Jake, who had his back to Huron, busted up laughing. Huron scratched his head as Jake whirled around. "Ha, now the joke's on you. Shoulda heard yourself."

Huron squinted. "Sometimes you're a real jerk, Jake."

"I know, but I figure we're even."

That night Aloha suffered a severe attack of insomnia. He snuck out of the house and went to his thinking spot to clear his head. He spent a few minutes reminiscing about the last two years, then the night grew bright with white light and the clouds dissolved, and in the light his mother appeared.

"My son," said the maiden of the sea. Her proud gaze centered on him.

He looked up at her, heart thudding. His eyes were aching as they drank in the sight. "Mom?"

"Aloha. I'm not only in heaven, we are one in the Holy Spirit. You have a light in you. Let it blaze within until the surface shines. Then you will truly be my successor."

He gasped, shocked that she had called him by his new nickname. Tears slid down his face. He was reminded freshly of the loss he'd come upon two years ago and of the time gone by.

"Mom, why do I have to carry this weight?" His voice was shaking. A thousand memories of the past came flooding back between their eyes.

"There are things that must be protected," she explained. "I love you, little sailor." The tears streamed down harder and faster. She'd just called him her special nickname for him.

"I love you, t-too," he stammered.

She put an arm around him and smiled. "I have to be quick. My time here is almost gone. You must use the sword God left for you to defeat Shakoda and The Goyle."

Aloha closed his eyes. "Who?"

"Shakoda. He is more than a boy. He's the summoner, and he wants to summon an evil creature known as The Goyle. You must use the sword to stop them. You'll know them when you meet them. Keep that sword handy. It will be useful when you face Barrett."

"Mother, how am I supposed to find Barrett?" he asked.

"God will lead you there. Don't worry so much," she told him. At this, her voice broke. She pulled him to her again and squeezed him more tightly. "Remember what you've been chosen for."

"Gotcha," he said. He tried to smile, but his lips kept fumbling for a way to express his grief.

She touched his forehead. Aloha stood speechless as she wiped her hand across his brow and said, "Believe and jump."

Aloha crinkled his nose, one eyebrow raised and one lowered. "What does that mean?" he asked.

She only smiled in return. "There is one more thing you must do."

"What's that?" Aloha questioned.

"You need to talk to Mari," she said. She faded away into grains of sand and was whisked into the ocean by a swift gust of wind.

"Goodbye, Mom," he said. He sniffled a few times.

Her voice came back to him at once, almost as an afterthought. Talk to Mari, she insisted. He came upon his friend as Mari was restlessly circling the bay. Mari had felt an aura of love coming from all around the area, like a warm caress surrounding him. The feeling vanished, and he was searching for the source when Aloha met up with him. Before Aloha could tell him of the spiritual experience he'd had with his mother, he made a grand discovery.

As he was walking toward the edge of the dock after hailing Mari, Aloha heard the sound of wind but could not feel it. He stopped as the wind suddenly picked up, swirling around him, making his clothes billow out behind him. His neatly groomed hair blew askew. Strangely, this wind did not affect the surroundings at all. And, Mari noted, it seemed to be coming not from outside of Aloha, but from within. Aloha smiled and closed his eyes. Heat rose in his chest. This is so cool, he thought, but what is this feeling? Suddenly the spirit of his father appeared, unnoticed by Aloha. He put his arms around his son and lifted him as Aloha jumped up. As the spirit held his son up, he beckoned to Mari. Why does he keep doing things like that, Mari wondered. He held out his fin but was too afraid to swim toward the ghost. Aloha laughed as what he perceived as the wind lifted him up, and he began to float.

"Wow, I'm floating again," Aloha exclaimed.

Puzzlement hid in his eyes, masked by his delight almost perfectly. Figures, Mari thought, everything good always happens to him. The spirit let his son go and flew under him with his back to the ground. Then he rolled over, grinned down at Mari, and saluted as he flew ahead of Aloha. He turned back to his son with a broad smile then disappeared. Aloha didn't see any of this.

"Mari, I'm flying," he shouted down.

"I can see that."

"I always wondered if I'd be able to fly like my mom did. I just thought that one time I floated in the air was a fluke. Guess not." He took off, zooming across the sky. He forgot all about his mother and what she had said for the time being.

Aloha was going to enjoy what he had for the moment. Why not, Mari thought. Were this approach to be used more often in life, change would be a lot less threatening. When approached as an adventure and a puzzle to fit together, life was easier to handle, or so he had found thus far. This made the world happy and fun. But when Aloha raced off without him, he felt like he was being left behind. While the kid was up there playing Peter Pan and watching the orcas spy-hopping a few miles to the west, he was stuck down here. Mari was about to go play somewhere else when Aloha came back and hovered over him. He stopped when he saw the hurt expression on Mari's face.

"What's wrong?"

"You can fly, and I can't. I don't like being left behind."

"Oh. Well, I'll slow down, and we can fly together."

"I can't fly," Mari pouted.

"Sure you can. All you got to do is jump. That's what I did. Then we can fly together."

"I have no idea what you're talking about."

"Just try it," he said.

Mari jumped into the air, and Aloha was beside him, imitating his leaps with his newfound ability. For a moment, their movements in water and air were a synchronized beat. They twisted and twirled through the clouds and swooped down, looping around each other as they traveled. Mari felt like he could fly between the stars, as though he personally knew each and every one. Aloha wrinkled his brow for a moment, then he opened his eyes wide. A flash of insight hit him.

He shouted, "I've got it."

"What?" Mari asked.

"I just realized something. The magic to fly comes from the imagination. If we both weren't imaginative, we wouldn't be able to fly now."

Mari's jaw dropped. "Why?" he inquired.

"Because that would be reality, but flying is make believe."

"I think I understand," Mari replied.

And so through the night they flew. Aloha used his power to keep Mari's skin wet as they traveled. They saw many great sights from orcas, blue whales, humpback whales, manatees, and seals, to a few stray wolves and cougars and alligators while flying over land. It's so nice to be able to get a better view of the land, Mari thought as they flew over Eden. He was amazed by the sensuous feel of the clouds against his skin, smooth and misty. They were perfect. The two of them really did touch the stars. They touched them with their hearts. The night ended, and the morning started on a happy note. They watched the bluish gray clouds turn to gold as the sun shone through the earth on its ascent. Soon the dawn was complete, and Aloha went home once more. Mari didn't see him again until that afternoon.

As Aloha approached, he said, "Mari, I have something important to tell you."

"Go on," Mari responded.

Aloha took a deep breath. "I had a visit from my mom last night."

"You did?"

"Yes. She came to me and told me that I am supposed to defeat an evil boy named Shakoda. He's supposed to have this creature with him called The Goyle. Then she wanted me to talk to you." Aloha paused.

"The Goyle," Mari gasped. "You must mean Shakoda the Summoner. I thought it was only a legend."

"You know about them too?"

"Yes. You said Shakoda is a boy, right?"

"Yeah." Aloha frowned.

"I think I may have met him."

"What?" Aloha croaked.

"A strange kid was watching me the other day, and then he said something snarky to me," Mari explained.

"What did he say?" Aloha asked.

"He said something like, 'You're time has come, guardian.' I have no clue what he meant by that."

"Why didn't you tell me about this?" Aloha asked. He huffed and rolled his eyes.

"Well, why didn't you tell me last night about what your mom said?" Mari challenged.

"I forgot when we were flying," he murmured.

"All right, all right. So you're gonna fight him?"

Aloha nodded. "Who is he, anyway?"

"According to myth, Shakoda is an evil spirit who wants to destroy the ocean so that he can create an eternal desert on earth. It was rumored that he was working on a creation to help him defeat the Son of the Waves. It was supposed to be a monster called The Goyle."

"Why does he want to create an eternal desert?" Aloha questioned.

"I don't know. Up until now, I thought it was just an old story."

"I see," Aloha said.

"Hey, Aloha, Mari," a voice called. They turned to see Jake and Huron approaching.

"Hi, guys," Aloha greeted.

"What's shaking, bacon?" Jake asked.

Aloha looked at Mari. "Should I tell them?"

"Should you tell us what?" Huron inquired.

Aloha filled them in about the visit from his mother, his discovery of flying, and how he was to battle the evil spirit Shakoda.

There was a pause as Jake and Huron took this in. Finally, Jake said, "Man, being the tide swooner sounds like such a drag."

"I'll never get used to all this weird supernatural stuff," grumbled Huron as he shook his head.

"This from the boy who can turn into a wolf," Jake replied, rolling his eyes. "All right, then. I guess we'd better help you prepare. Huron, go wolf and fetch the crowbar from under the deck."

"Why?" Huron asked.

"So you can spar with him, duh."

Huron glared at him, then transformed and raced off. He brought the crowbar back in less than five minutes. Jake patted his head and cooed, "Good boy." Huron snapped his jaws at him before turning back into a human.

They took turns sparring with Aloha, using the crowbar. Their weapons clashed fiercely, and Aloha noted that Huron was very sure of himself. He fought with the determination of a master, as though he'd been trained. Aloha wondered if he had taken fencing lessons. After about an hour, he defeated his brother. He barely made it, but he managed to knock the crowbar from Huron's hand. Huron beamed at him. Aloha panted, sweat dripping down his face. They took a break after he beat Huron.

"Huron?" Aloha asked.

"Yeah?"

"How did you get so skilled at fencing?"

He grinned. "I was in kendo for two years back in Minnesota."

"Oh." Aloha was thrilled. "What about you, Jake? Wanna go?"

"Uh, well, I wasn't exactly good at—"

"He's a lover, not a fighter," Huron interjected.

"Exactly," Jake agreed.

Mari snickered. The idea of Jake fighting anyone was unreal.

"Oh, shut up, you beast," Jake retorted.

Mari stuck his tongue out at him.

"You're still gonna help me practice, right, Jake?" Aloha intruded.

"Of course. It would, like, be my privilege."

"Teenagers," Aloha said, rolling his eyes at Jake's use of the word *like*.

"What?" Jake asked defensively.

"We need an English-to-teen translator," teased Huron.

Jake grabbed the crowbar. "Let's go, hot shot," he muttered to Aloha.

They sprung to action. Jake's stance was all wrong. His movements were awkward and rushed. Jake over-exaggerated his swings and missed with his thrusts, ducking at inappropriate intervals. He looked like he was doing a movie fight scene or something. His attempt was ludicrous. It didn't matter. Aloha beat him with quiet efficiency.

"I'll fight you again, if you want," Huron offered.

"Let's do this thing," was Aloha's response.

Aloha performed as well as Hamlet in his battle with Laertes. Huron, however, did not fare so well. Aloha's skill had increased tenfold, and Huron lost almost immediately. He fell to the ground, gawping up at Aloha.

"Holy donkeys," he said loudly.

"Aw dude, and you were griping about my vocabulary," Jake complained.

"Well done, tide swooner," came a nasty voice from behind them.

"I should have known. Evil has a way of fouling up a place," Mari said with a sneer.

"Be silent, guardian," barked the demonic creature.

"Shakoda the Summoner," Aloha declared through clenched teeth.

"So you know my name. I've been watching you train. I see you're finally ready to fight me. The battle will commence at midnight."

"You've been watching me? That's a little weird," Aloha said.

"I was waiting for you to ready yourself for battle," claimed Shakoda.

"But, couldn't you have just attacked me?"

"There are rules against that. The Creator forbids it." When Shakoda said "Creator," a cantankerous glint of distaste came into his eyes.

"What's your beef with me?" Aloha asked.

"I will defeat you, tide swooner. When I finish this task for my master, he will grant me dominion over the sea. And I will destroy it and all its inhabitants. Then the land these waters once occupied will become a desert."

"Your master?" Aloha queried, confused.

"His name is feared more than any other among villains. They say he is the source of evil. His name is Barrett."

"Barrett," Aloha grunted, scowling.

"I take it you've heard of him," Shakoda returned.

"Oh, I know of him, yes." Something occurred to him. "Why do you want to destroy the ocean and create a desert, anyway?"

"Destruction and corruption. These are the goals of all evil creatures."

"But why?"

"Because that's what evil beings do."

"But why?"

"Insolent brat. Because it's evil, and evil beings do evil things."

"That doesn't seem like a very good reason to me. Why're you evil?"

"Because I choose to be."

"Why?"

"It's fun," Shakoda shot back. On his face was a look of shock at Aloha's audacity. Aloha didn't even get the next "Why?" out before Shakoda answered, "The power. The glorious power of ruining creation."

"Have you ever tried being good?" countered Aloha.

"No," Shakoda admitted.

"Well then, how do you know you wouldn't think *that's* fun?"

"Foolish child. What makes you think I want to know what being good is like?"

"I don't know. I was just asking."

"Why were you asking?" He spat this question out viciously.

"I was curious."

"But why were you curious?"

"I don't know."

"Why don't you know?"

"I just don't." If Shakoda had hoped to annoy Aloha the way Aloha had him, he was very disappointed. Aloha started to ask him another question, but he disappeared.

"Harsh," Jake said.

Aloha burst out laughing. "Did you see the look on his face? His face was all red and puffy. Cherry red, that's what I oughta call him." Pretty soon he had all of them chortling.

Aloha stopped laughing, and an awkward silence descended over them. Huron looked at him. "You guys wanna ride bikes or something for a while?"

"I guess. I certainly don't feel like surfing or swimming, no offense, Mari," Aloha said.

"None taken."

"Jake, you coming?" Huron asked.

"No, I'll stay with Mari. He probably shouldn't be alone either, just in case that guy comes back. Aloha, remember to take your sword. Huron, take the crowbar with you."

Huron and Aloha nodded.

"Good," Jake said.

Aloha started home to get his bike, and Jake said to Huron, "Make sure you two stay together."

Huron nodded. "Do you want to go with him instead? You're stronger than I am."

"I know, but you're better with a sword. That'll come in handy if you encounter that freak again."

"All right." Huron ran to catch up with Aloha.

Jake looked at Mari with faraway eyes.

"Jake?"

"What?" he responded, disengaged.

"Wanna go for a swim?" Mari asked. He didn't know what else to do to occupy their minds.

"Sure," Jake agreed nonchalantly.

"Beat you to the dock," Mari called.

"Whatever." Jake swam off after him. They raced to the dock, and Mari won easily. "You won," Jake muttered.

Meanwhile, Huron and Aloha rode their bikes around Siesta Key without much conversation. They cruised down the sidewalk near the spot where Aloha had first met Mari, then biked back to Turtle Beach, parked their bikes, and sat for a bit, watching the waves.

"Huron, this is boring. Want to go explore Eden?"

Huron sighed. "Sure, why not?"

The boys made their way over the decrepit rope bridge. They reached the other side and traveled into the thick forest. Aloha used his sword to hack a path for them. Huron remained silent and detached.

"Check it out, Huron. I'm Doctor Livingstone," Aloha announced.

"I wonder what we'll find," Huron said.

"Dunno."

That ended their brief conversation. They continued until they reached a tangle of plants and shrubs that blocked their path. Aloha huffed, kicked at the brush, and turned around. His hands were quaking.

"Come on, Huron. Let's go back."

"All right. It's starting to get dark, anyway."

Soon the sun set, and darkness rushed down the beach. Not a word was said as the boys entered the house, anxious with dread. Midnight rolled around pretty quickly, and none of them had slept. Aloha made them promise to stay at home. Jake and Huron agreed reluctantly. He left them in charge of covering for him in case their parents woke up. Tails even tried to follow him out of the house, whimpering with concern, but Aloha made Huron grab him. He slipped swiftly out the sliding door.

The waves broke harshly against the shore. The sea was churning with excitement, spilling itself onto the land. The sky was a majestic purple tinged with a violent red. Aloha held out his arms and motioned the waves to slow until they calmed. He unsheathed his sword and began warming up for the battle. *Father, help me. I want to protect everything,* he prayed. Mari observed from a spot where Aloha couldn't see. He had made a promise to stay a good distance from the battleground, which he didn't, of course.

"At last," came the greedy voice of Shakoda.

"I'm ready," Aloha informed him, eyes narrowed.

"First you will deal with my creation. If you live, you will fight me. If you survive that, then you'll have saved your precious ocean."

Aloha lifted his sword. "Bring it on."

Smirking, Shakoda flipped backward in the air until he landed on a dock post. Aloha looked up at him, baffled. Shakoda raised his arms into the air, palms bent upward. He began chanting. His voice was raising something, summoning. Aloha watched in awe as a form began to appear in the air. His eyes about popped out. It had the body of a panther but with certain differences. It stood upright and wore a maroon cape, and its snout was shaped like a dragon's. It had two elongated nostrils. Where a panther's paws would be, it had hands and feet that were mostly claws. On the top of its head was a red crest with three oddly shaped horns coming out of it. It roared ferociously.

Aloha didn't bat an eye. He soared straight into battle. The creature didn't have wings, but it could fly—sort of. Really, it just sort of floated aloft, waiting eagerly for Aloha to attack. It was then that he noticed the terrible smell coming off the beast. It was the smell of sulfur.

Sword poised, Aloha rushed at The Goyle. The Goyle swatted at him with its huge clawed hands. Its claws were about half as long as Aloha. He ducked, weaving in and out of its grip from the gaps between its claws. He shot forward under the beast's arm and stabbed it in the side. The creature bellowed in pain, but did not back down. Instead, it looked over at Mari. With a grin, it slapped Aloha, connecting with him in midair, and knocked him into the sea. As he fell, Aloha's mouth went slack, and his eyes rolled back in his head. No, Mari thought. No! He sped over to Aloha and pulled him to the surface. The boy was unconscious. Mari tried to wake him by echoing in his ear, but it was no use. Behind him, he could hear Shakoda's ghoulish, underhanded laugh. Suddenly Mari felt a searing pain in his sides.

"Ah!" he wailed as The Goyle's claws squeezed him.

It lifted Mari to its malevolent golden eye's level and glared at him. As it opened its mouth wide, its hand moved him toward that direction. Oh crud, Mari thought, not only am I a goner, but now I know where that rank smell was coming from—and I really didn't want to know that. He must have screamed without being aware of it, because below him Aloha's eyes snapped open, and he looked up weakly and saw Mari. The Goyle's grip tightened, and Mari went limp in its arms. He blanked out for a few moments, but Aloha heard him repeat the words, "The sword. Use the sword. Now." over and over.

"Mari," his friend whispered painfully, "hang on. Please. I can't lose you. I won't."

Mari's eyes moved unconsciously until Aloha was in view. He had heard him, though he wasn't sure how. Aloha's whisper had been too low to be audible from this distance. Mari came to and looked at him. Aloha was up and fighting. He was fast and violent. He stabbed the beast in one arm, in one eye, and in the stomach. His sword was hitting the monster on the mark every time but, to his horror, its wounds were healing themselves. Aloha stabbed the arm that held his friend, and The Goyle discarded Mari casually, dropping him unceremoniously into the ocean. Mari's breathing was ragged as he plummeted, tumbling over himself a few times, down to the sea.

He hit the waves hard and was almost knocked out again. Vaguely, he became aware of something catching him underneath the water. He looked up and spotted the spirit of Aloha's father. The spirit was holding him. Oh yeah, Mari thought, he couldn't catch me before I got the charley horse. The spirit dragged Mari to the surface. Shakoda watched the battle with great interest and his best and brightest evildoer leer.

Aloha was dodging the monster's fierce hands, hammering at the claws with his sword in an attempt to relieve the creature of them, and trying to watch out for its thrashing tail, which was like a whip. He flew up to avoid the tail, landed on top of the monster's fist, and slashed relentlessly at one claw, hacking and hacking. Mari could see that Aloha was forming a strategy. When he figured it out, he soared upward all the way to the top of the creature's head, moving so fast that he was a blur. Skirting the reaching claws and the horns on the crest, he landed and worked on cutting off the monster's horns, two of which were up to his shoulder. The middle horn was taller than he was. The Goyle was snarling, clearly unhappy. When it opened its mouth to roar, Mari saw something: a large, black hole on the roof of its mouth.

"Aloha. Go for the hole inside his mouth. You must use your sword."

Mari wondered if this injury might be The Goyle's weakness. He glanced over at Shakoda with a simpering smile. We'll beat you yet, he thought. Then Mari started as Shakoda turned his eyes from the battle and flicked them over to him, scowling savagely as he pointed at Mari. Why's he threatening me? I did nothing, Mari thought. Meanwhile, Aloha turned and pulled his sword out of the groove in the horn he had cut and nodded. A large clawed hand closed around his small being. Mari gasped. Aloha was trapped inside the creature's fist. Father, please help me get out of this one, he prayed.

Mari heard Shakoda exhale sharply in fear and wonder when the beast cried in pain a moment later, its eyes widening, pupils turning into a slit. A hole followed by the blade of Aloha's sword emerged between two of its claws. A chunk dropped out of them, and Aloha thrust the sword out. He climbed face-first out of its grip, raising the sword to defend himself as he did so. While the monster was distracted by its own blood, Aloha flew up into its mouth with a look of disgust as he caught scent of the evil aroma. He shuddered—and Mari thought he said, "Gross!" as a big drop of drool dripped off of one of its teeth onto him—and stabbed it in the hole, craftily avoiding being eaten or chewed as he dodged about.

The Goyle yammered as gooey sprays of blood and bits of flesh rained down, its body shattering into several fragments which disappeared into the great royal purple of the sky. Shakoda was stunned. He glared at Mari then at Aloha, who was covered with blood and saliva.

"Looks like that monster needed a breath mint and a trip to the dentist," Aloha said as he wiped himself off.

"I've never been fond of dentists," Shakoda replied absently. "All right, boy. You still have to prove yourself to me."

But Aloha smiled and shook his head, sending droplets of drool and blood hurtling through the air. He lunged at Shakoda, who eluded him and went for Mari, thundering, "Guardian, you die now."

Mari jumped up as the Summoner sailed toward him and smacked him with his tail fluke. Shakoda grabbed his cheek, growling. Aloha quickly got between them, a sour expression on his face. With that, he lifted his sword until the stars reflected on the cool blade. He shot forward so fast that Shakoda failed to see him. The next thing he knew, the point of Aloha's sword was resting against his throat. Although he looked afraid, Shakoda laughed.

"You can't kill me that way."

Aloha raised his eyebrows. An indignant expression scrawled itself onto Shakoda's face. Aloha ignored this. He pulled the sword back and thrust it upward again.

"Come up and take what is yours," Aloha bellowed.

Before Shakoda could figure out what Aloha was doing, the waves rose up in a spiral and snatched him. Shakoda was sinking into the ocean, unable to get out.

"The sea knows her enemies, and she isn't kind to those who challenge her protectors," Aloha said firmly to the rapidly disappearing Shakoda. "You are banished forever to the craters of the sea. Daylight you shall never again see."

Shakoda screamed in horror as he was swallowed. *He's going to be hot with all that magma down there*, Mari thought. After listening to a lot of caterwauling, shrieking, and idle threats, they saw the last of the Summoner. The Son of the Waves and his friend sighed in relief.

"You okay?" Mari asked.

"Yeah. The Lord had it covered. What about you?"

"I'm fine," Mari told him.

Aloha hugged the battered dolphin.

"It's a good thing for the sea creatures that God gave you that power."

Aloha howled with laughter. "Yeah, but it's an even better thing that He used it for me. Like I had a clue what I was doing. I asked Him for help, just like my mom used to do."

"Really?" Mari frowned, wondering what it was like to pray.

"Of course."

"You'd better get home, Aloha."

"I know. See ya."

"Goodnight, little sailor," Mari whispered.

Aloha went home, longing to sleep, but Jake and Huron kept him up all night by asking him to tell them how he defeated Shakoda and the evil Goyle. That is, after they forced him to shower.

Transformation

A lovely sunset painting was draped across the sky. The artist had brushed through the sun's golden light with red and pink and purple. These colors fringed the great blue sky above them. Twilight was approaching when Mari saw them: dolphins swimming playfully out in the navy blue water, some jumping high, others leaping through the surf. As the pod, his estranged family, went by, he called to them, and they swam faster. He tailed them for a while, mostly out of boredom, until Alpha dolphin noticed him. He glowered at Mari.

"Get out of here. You no longer belong with us."

Mari exhaled sharply, water shooting out of his blowhole. The wound in his heart reopened. His heart throbbed with shuddersome force. "It's a free ocean. I can swim where I want," he sputtered.

"Family," Alpha called, "let's go."

Mari looked around, taking in the surroundings. It struck him that they were headed for dangerous water. The pod was nearing Eden. The whirlpool alone would batter them, if not kill them. Its force would throw them against the sharp rocks that were just out from the shore and along the bridge. If one knew how to navigate around that, one might be okay, but there were also some tiger sharks in the area—nasty, gutsy ones.

"Wait! You're going toward—"

Alpha dolphin turned back. "Quiet, you!"

"Do you have a death wish? Because that's what'll happen if you—"

"And what would you know about it, hmmm?" he roared.

Mari got the implication: they thought that he would have caused their deaths by associating with humans had they not exiled him. He saw the rest of the dolphins move on ahead of them. He bolted through the water to the front of the line. They glared at him as he passed by.

"Stop. Humans are near here," he shouted. They all froze. At last, one of them spoke up.

"Get out of our way."

"Listen to me. If you don't want to be killed, listen."

"This better be good, outcast, or you'll be sorry."

"You're going near Eden. There is a horrible whirlpool and shallow water with jagged rocks. Stay away from there."

"That's enough. We move forward. And as for you, you must leave." Mari hadn't noticed Alpha dolphin coming up behind him.

"But you'll get them all killed."

He ignored Mari, and they headed forward. Mari followed. Alpha's swimming right toward the whirlpool, he thought.

"No, don't," Mari bawled.

A jolt of energy shot through him, and he flew through the water and knocked Alpha dolphin out of the way. They just missed getting sucked into the whirlpool. The other dolphins eyed them with a mixture of fear and surprise. Alpha turned to rush at Mari, assuming that he was challenging him.

One of the pod edged in front of him, saying, "Stop. He saved you from that whirlpool." Alpha looked back toward where he had been swimming. He recognized the danger. "Let us talk in private," he commanded, and the rest of the pod swam away. He looked hard at Mari. "Why would you save us? What do you care?"

Mari looked away. "Dolphins' code of honor," he murmured.

The expression of wonderment on Alpha's face was almost comical. Mari could almost hear Alpha thinking, Maybe I was wrong about you. The elder dolphin's eyes quickly narrowed, and he regained his usual gruff expression.

"Well, there's nothing I can do for you, so…" He began to leave.

"Wait," Mari yelled. "Tell me how my parents died. Tell me something about them. You owe it to me."

"I don't know what happened to them."

"You're lying," Mari sniveled.

"No."

"Why are you always hiding things from me? Tell me the truth, now," he demanded.

"The truth is, the maiden brought you to us and told us to care for you, but she never told us what happened to your pod. She did mention that one day you were to return to where you came from."

So that was what she did for me, he thought. "What did she mean by that?"

"I don't know, and I don't think she did, either."

"So she left you to care for me, but you never loved me like the others. Why?"

"You're too wild, too different."

"That's why you hate me?"

"You don't belong here. You don't belong with us."

Mari's anger boiled over. He charged forward and hit Alpha with the tip of his nose. "After what I just did for you, you still won't accept me. I hate you."

Alpha said nothing as he left Mari.

That night Mari swept tumultuously through the seas. The uncertainty of his origins fueled his crazed movement. Meanwhile, Aloha was asleep in his bed. Huron snored away across the room, cozy in his own bed.

Tails slept on the floor beside his bed. He had just shifted position when a sound and a rather sulfuric, dirty smell awoke him. He sniffed harder and picked up the aroma of the

Minnesota forest where he'd met Huron. He jerked his head up. Both the scents and the weird sound, like the scratching of nails on wood, came from across the room near Aloha's bed. Something hunched, hairy, and green was looming over Aloha as he slept. A quick survey of the room revealed an open window, presumably through which this thing had entered. Tails lowered his ears and growled. The creature scraped something along the curve of Aloha's face and lifted him up with one arm. It tucked the sleeping boy underneath its arm. Tails barked. Huron startled awake and murmured, "What's going on, boy?"

He and Tails had time to notice that the creature had rolled Aloha up in his bedspread like a burrito before the thing became a cackling blur moving toward the window. Tails chased after them, but the creature hurtled through the window and out of sight. Huron got up and ran to the window as Jake opened the bedroom door and entered.

"What was that freakish scratching noise?" Jake asked, yawning.

"I don't know."

"Where's Aloha? And why'd Tails bark?"

"Some bizarre little monster just grabbed Aloha and took him out the window." Huron didn't see the blank look on his brother's face. He was leaning out the window, scanning the distance. Aloha and the thing were nowhere to be seen.

Jake's eyes went wide. Something just kidnapped my brother, he thought. He ignored his pressing need to go to the bathroom.

"Jake, why don't you go find Mari? Maybe he knows a legend about whatever that thing is that will help us out. Tails and I will go look for Aloha. Okay?"

Jake said, "All right."

The wind was low, just a small breeze. The air was cleansing and fresh. Mari took a deep breath and looked up to the sky, searching the infinite blue depths. Where do I come from, and why was I taken from there? He closed his eyes for a moment.

His echo location told him that something was approaching. A vision of a pirate ship came unbidden into his thoughts, and he wondered what treasures it was planning to steal from him. He heard the sounds of the waves lapping against the sides of a boat and opened his eyes. A ship was making passage against the night. Mari turned back toward shore. He heard several muffled thuds and moved toward the sound.

Out of the darkness came Jake. He ran in short, brisk strides into the water, panting. Mari blew out his breath in a harsh gasp. The way Jake's eyes were flicking back and forth drew his attention. Unease stabbed through him. Jake stopped to catch his breath, his chest hitching madly, his face a mixture of exhaustion and fear. Mari almost begged him not to speak.

"Aloha's gone. I heard a freakish scratching noise on my way to the bathroom, and I went into Huron and Aloha's room to see what it was. I didn't see Aloha. Huron told me some weird creature took him," he began and stopped. He gulped in air and informed Mari that Huron and Tails were out trying to find him. "Mari, do you know what this monster was? Is there some kind of legend about it?"

"No. There aren't legends about this sort of thing. Not that I've heard, anyway."

Jake looked at him, pleading for something even he couldn't understand. Mari paused, thinking. "Go get Huron, and we'll see what we can figure out."

"Right," he said obediently and left.

As he waited for them, Mari stared upward again. Who would have taken him? He listened to the lonely roaring of the sea surrounding him. He closed his eyes, and the world was spinning. At first all he could see was darkness. Where am I, he thought. He looked around and, suddenly, a light glanced off the side of a rocky structure. A stalactite. So he was in a cave. He saw the light move, and it highlighted something. Mari watched a silhouette writhing, struggling against something. Then the light revealed it clearly.

This time, he saw Aloha bound with tight rawhide strips in a very dark cavern. The image was slightly blurred. Mari watched his eyes close in resignation, his head drooping, his skin pale. He looked like a corpse sitting in a crypt. Within the bowels of darkness, Mari could see a stalagmite sticking up from the ground. Without warning, Aloha's head snapped up, and his eyes opened wide. Fear and hope came simultaneously into those transparencies of the soul. The vision evaporated before Mari's eyes. Someone's coming, he thought, his attention drawn back to the shore. Huron emerged from over the hill. He was followed by Jake. Huron came into the sea and hugged Mari.

"You have any idea how to help us find Aloha, Mari?"

"I'm not sure."

"Yeah, Jake said you didn't know any legends this time."

"I might know something, but tell me what happened first."

"Tails and I saw some shady green thing come and take him. When Tails tried to help, the thing disappeared through the window. What is it you know?"

"I think he's in a cave somewhere."

Jake gawked at Mari, and Huron's jaw dropped. He and Jake glanced back and forth at each other. "You can't know that," Huron cried.

"I'm telling you, he's in a cave," Mari insisted.

"Why do you think that?" Jake asked.

"I saw a vision of him."

Huron furrowed his brow at this but said nothing. Jake looked befuddled. "A vision? You saying you're psychic?"

"I don't think so, but I did see a vision of him in a cave. I don't know where the cave is located, though."

Jake opened his mouth as if to speak, then closed it instead and shook his head.

Huron frowned. Then his eyes lit up. "Oh yeah, Tails thinks he may end up in Minnesota, because the thing that took him reeked of Minnesota forest."

"Okay, so what're we gonna do?" Mari asked.

Neither Jake nor Huron answered. Both were mulling over the options in their heads. Mari looked back and forth at them then realized he couldn't answer this question either. His thoughts were whirling, and he heard Huron and Jake cry out in surprise. Huron dropped his hands to his sides and backed away. Jake stood rooted to his spot, gaping. Mari began to feel an odd sense of lightness, and along with that came another spinning sensation. His stomach seemed to drop out, making him lightheaded. He opened his eyes, aware that he was being lifted; he hovered in the air. His vision clouded over, and he felt his body bounce up and down a little. Then he was stable. His vision cleared. Mari looked around to see if maybe Aloha's father's spirit was holding him up, but he didn't see anything.

In a deep pocket of his mind, layers of distrust peeled back for just a moment, and he was connected to the spiritual world. A link had formed between he and his Creator. A warm contentment washed over him. His surroundings churned. The sea *whooshed*, and the waves broke hard. He looked down at Huron, who had wonderment in his eyes. All around Mari were spirals of golden light. A white light eclipsed his surroundings and, in a flash, he was dropped feet first on the ground. When he saw the sand beneath him, he panicked. I've beached myself, he thought. Automatically, he reached up with one hand and pushed aside a strand of hair. He was too confused to notice what had happened.

"Huron, Jake, can you help me get back in the water?" he asked, his voice breaking. Jake did not reply. He was making funny gurgling noises. Huron opened his mouth to speak and closed it, unable to form the words. Mari gazed at him in awe. I'm above eye level with him, his mind exclaimed. And the sea looked a lot lower all of a sudden. Whoa, he thought. He looked down at himself and discovered with a shriek that he had become human. He had arms and legs, clothes and shoes. Mari saw that he was wearing a dark blue shirt that was unbuttoned to reveal a yellow

T-shirt underneath and black shorts with a white drawstring. Around his neck was a magenta necklace with a shark's tooth on the end, and around his wrist was magenta bracelet with a charm hanging off the end of it. The charm was in the shape of a cross.

Huron smiled and said, "You look very handsome, Mari."

"Huron, I…whoa, my voice is so much deeper."

"He's almost as studly as I am," bragged Jake.

Ignoring him, Huron said, "Hmmm, you look about fourteen years old. I guess that age would be right for you, wouldn't you say?" A calculating expression appeared on his face.

"Uh, yeah, sure." Mari began laughing as a thought struck him.

"What? What is it?"

"Huron, you're a lot shorter than you used to be."

"Nah. You just never had the guts to hightail your lazy fins up here and impress me with your height. Although I would have thought with your massive girth as a dolphin that you'd be more muscled now. Look at you; you're like a toothpick."

"Shut up. I haven't had time to work out. I've only been human for about sixty seconds."

"See? Human for sixty seconds, and already he's making excuses," Jake joked.

Huron broke out into peals of laughter. Then he motioned Mari to the water's glassy edge. "Look at yourself, Mari."

Mari stumbled toward the water, drawing childish giggles from Huron. He found it awkward to walk on land. It was the most wonderful, frustrating, and difficult form of movement he could think of short of having to learn to leap like a gazelle. He wasn't used to having so many joints, either. Mari staggered, caught his balance then overbalanced. He fell down several times in the ten feet from the shore to the water, but by the last two feet, he had mastered it quite well. Jake favored him with a look of hilarity.

"Aw, our little Mari's growing up so fast, Huron. He's already learned to walk," Jake cooed.

Mari chose to ignore him. Standing tall and moving as fluidly as a newly dolphin-turned-human could, he reached the water's edge. He stared at his reflection. His first thought was, Oh, great, I have strange hair, too. Then he wondered why he had hair similar—though darker and with black mixed in—in color to Jake's and very dark eyes similar to his as well.

"Wow," he exclaimed.

Excited as he was, he couldn't escape the question that immediately came to mind. What does this mean? Mari grew quiet, and for a moment, he started to feel weak. This must be what it's like to be drowsy, he thought. He had never been so tired in his life. He couldn't have afforded to be, given that dolphins didn't sleep very long. Mari had seen the midnight hours, the sun-fire mornings, and everything in between.

"Penny for your thoughts, Mari?" Jake said.

"Just taking in the fact that I'm human." He shuffled his feet anxiously.

"Psh, that's boring. We gotta figure out a way to rescue Aloha."

"Well, what's your suggestion?" Huron snapped.

"We should go back to the house and get some rest, then head out tomorrow morning."

"We should go now," Huron said.

"Yes, but if we know he's in Minnesota near our old home, then we can get some bus tickets and take the bus to Minnesota, so we wouldn't have to walk. Then you can go wolf and track Aloha's scent. We'll find the cave for sure."

"Good idea," Mari said.

"It's too bad that you don't have your car this week, Jake," Huron said.

Mari looked at him. "Why doesn't he have his car?"

"My dad's buddy is borrowing his car, so he's using mine for work," Jake explained.

"What about your mom's car?"

"Dude, she needs it to go to work too."

"Oh."

"Bus tickets it is," Huron chimed in.

"Tomorrow after Mom and Dad leave for work, we'll go to the bank and the bus station."

"Okay. Come on, Mari, let's go," Huron said, grabbing his arm.

They led him back to the house and sneaked in through the kitchen door. Huron and Mari parted ways with Jake at his room and proceeded to Huron's room, where Tails waited for them. His wet, brown eyes fell on Mari, and he licked Mari's hand sympathetically. His tail wagged slowly. Mari petted him. Jake and Huron fell into a fretful sleep, but he lay in Aloha's bed, unable to sleep. He was definitely tired. His eyes kept closing and opening. He wasn't used to having eyelashes and eyebrows. They kept tickling his fingers when he ran them across his face, amazed by the sensation of being human. He saw Tails curl up beside Huron and drift off peacefully. Mari flopped onto his back. He angled the pillow to get better lift then looked up.

He pictured Aloha as he stared at the ceiling and shivered, pulling his overshirt closed and buttoning it. At last he rose from the bed and slunk downstairs to the kitchen. He opened the sliding door, glided out onto the deck, and shut it quietly behind him. He walked down the stairs and through the sand and stumbled up the hill to the sacred place where Aloha always meditated. Mari sat down. Sand clung to his shorts and dusted his shins. *Aloha*, he thought, *I can't do this. I need someone to guide me.*

"Can anyone hear me? I'm looking for my friend. I need to find him."

Mari stared inquiringly at the stars that were scattered between the clouds. It occurred to him that he didn't know whom he was questioning. Was he praying, asking God for help? *Maybe I am*, he thought. A flicker of brightness skated across his face. *What is that light*, he wondered. He didn't expect an answer, yet he felt that someone should answer. His eyes shifted from that pocket of stars to the bluish tinted cloud that was stretched out above. The source of the light was coming from behind the cloud. The cloud was illuminated suddenly, conflicting with the sky around it. The cloud gave way as the shape of a man phased through. Mari swallowed hard. He recognized the man. It was Aloha's father.

"Hello, Mari. I'm glad we finally have a chance to talk," said the spirit.

"You're Aloha's father," Mari declared.

The spirit nodded. "Mm hm."

"Why do you keep appearing? What do you want with me?" Mari asked. His chest tightened, and his throat closed. Hurt filled his eyes.

"Because you need me. And I'm here."

"What kind of answer is that?" Mari shot back. He tilted his head to the side, brow furrowed.

"If you want to help Aloha, then you must do two things," the spirit continued.

"What's that?" Mari asked.

"First, trust yourself. And for the second task, you'll need to get the dagger."

"What then?"

"You'll have to use the dagger in battle."

Mari gaped. Before he could respond, the spirit began to fade. "Wait," Mari called.

As Aloha's father vanished into the surrounding vapors, his eyes sparkled. His expression was fraught with meaning. Mari got up. He knew what he had to do. He went back to the house and crawled underneath the deck, digging in the sand until he found the rusty dagger. He picked it up, eyeing it with dismay. He had never really liked the thing. It seemed dangerous. But now was the time to put personal preferences aside. He took the dagger into the house with him. When he got back upstairs, Huron was still asleep.

He sat on the bed for a moment. Out of the corner of his eye, he spotted Aloha's backpack. The bag was blue with brown suede on the bottom. That's the same one he had when I found him, he thought. These days he carried a different book bag. In fact, Mari was sure he'd never used this one again after he had gotten adopted. He slowly stepped over to the bag. He bent down, peering intently at it. Should he look in there and see what Aloha had been carrying on that fateful morning when they met? Mari grabbed it and hurried back to the bed. He yanked the zipper open, bursting with curiosity. But as he peered into the dimness inside the bag, he felt an unease that puzzled him. He tried to ignore it and reached his hand into the interior. His fingers stopped just centimeters short of a piece of paper. More precisely, an envelope. I can't do this, he realized. Somehow, he was not yet ready to learn whatever secrets the bag possessed. It was with a disappointed and troubled heart that he pulled the zipper shut again.

Where am I, Aloha thought, looking around. His head throbbed so badly that he could barely open his eyes. He tried to move his hands so he could massage his temples and bit his lips to stifle a scream of pain. Leather straps bound his hands together at the wrists. He lifted his arms anyway and tried rubbing his forehead with his fingers. There was darkness all around him, but for a moment, for just a brief moment, a circle of light filled a small spot in the distance. It shimmered brightly at the edges, and inside the circle, he saw the night sky filled with clouds and the beach and…a boy. Aloha choked on his breath. That's Turtle Beach, he realized. He continued to observe the beach and the stranger through the lens of the portal. The sky in this world was navy blue with light bluish-gray clouds. The shape of the portal was still circular, but the outline was in liquid-fluid motion, rippling like a mud puddle. The image contained within had the vivid wetness of a reflection in water. Aloha gasped when he saw Jake and Huron walk into view next to the unknown boy and strained to open his eyes wider. Huron, Jake, here I am, Aloha wanted to shout.

He deliberately focused on the strange kid again. The kid was tall with dark blue and black hair in an odd, cartoonish style. He was shifting his feet up and down. This boy was talking with his brothers. He couldn't hear what they were saying, but the conversation looked exciting. The new boy's hair blew back in a sudden gust of wind, and the strands were pushed in wild directions.

Whoever he was, Aloha liked his getup. He wore a yellow T-shirt with a blue button-down shirt over it, black drawstring shorts, and wickedly cool blue, yellow, and white tennis shoes. He also had a shark's tooth necklace and a bracelet with a cross-shaped charm hanging off of it. The way the boy was shuffling his feet reminded Aloha of Mari's nervous habit of moving his fluke up and down. Aloha sucked in a ragged breath. He exhaled with a sob as he watched the portal of light and the world within begin to vanish. The reality of his confinement hit him. Aloha struggled against his restraints, but it was no use.

All right, he told himself, don't panic. Huron and Jake will find me somehow. Tears spilled down his cheeks. I don't even know where I am, so how are they going to know? He hung his head and closed his eyes, preferring internal darkness to external. His mind flashed back to that boy who was with Jake and Huron. They certainly didn't look too sad that I'm gone, he thought. Aloha opened his eyes and glared into the darkness. They can't replace me with that kid. The pain in his head worsened. Aloha groaned. He still couldn't remember how he'd ended up in this pit. At some point he fell asleep.

Mari stuffed the dagger in Aloha's backpack and lay down again. When the sunrise came, he heard Jake slip into the room.

"Mari, you need to come with me. You'll stay in the basement until my parents leave," Jake whispered.

"Okay."

Mari followed Jake down to the basement. He sat on the couch, daydreaming. A couple of hours later, Jake went to wake Huron. Mari heard them rattling around in the kitchen as they made breakfast for their parents. About twenty minutes later, creaking and groaning noises startled him as Jimmy and Marisol came down the stairs and sauntered into the kitchen. This was followed by a muffled exclaim of surprise.

"You made us breakfast?" came through the floor. Mari smiled as he listened to the faint bustle of a family in the morning. The racket dissolved into a deep silence that made him uneasy. He relaxed when he head Jake say, "Aloha's still sleeping."

Mari only heard enough of Jimmy's response to deduce that he wanted Jake to tell Aloha not to make a habit of sleeping in. This was confirmed when he heard Jake's nervous, screechy response: "Okay, I'll tell him."

When at last Jimmy and Marisol were gone, Mari crept up to see Jake and Huron cooking something else. "I thought you already made breakfast?"

"We made our parents breakfast. Me and Huron wanted something else. Besides, I assume you're hungry too."

"Yeah. While you're doing that, is it okay if I get a shower?" I should at least start this trip off being clean, he thought.

"Sure," Huron said, "bathroom's this way."

"Thanks," Mari told him.

He entered the bathroom and closed the door. He did exactly as he remembered Aloha having done when he showered at the beach. He took off his shirt and socks and got in the shower. This was quite an awkward thing for him, having never showered before, but he managed to fare. When he finished, he grabbed Aloha's sword, tied the strap to the backpack, and went into the kitchen. Jake and Huron looked at him with very large eyes. Huron was the first to speak.

"Uh, Mari, did you spill something on your shorts?" he asked.

"No, I just took a shower."

Huron and Jake exchanged looks and snickered. He grew annoyed. Why did they laugh at everything he did? He could be human. Really, he could.

"What?" he asked, dumbfounded.

"You saw Aloha use the beach shower, didn't you?" Jake guessed.

"Yeah, so?"

"Oh, nothing." Mari glared at them.

"Yeah, that pretty much explains it," Huron added with a grin.

Mari raised an eyebrow but decided not to comment. They ate a breakfast of eggs and bacon with a side of toast. After they were done eating, they cleaned up the kitchen, washed and dried the dishes, and put them away. Before they left, Jake asked Huron if they should write a note. Huron nodded. Jake wrote it and signed his name. Mari grabbed the pen when he was finished. Jake snatched the pen out of his hand and scolded him.

"No, Mari. *You're* not supposed to sign it. Huron, sign for Aloha."

Huron signed his name then Aloha's. Then he perused the note and cast a sarcastic glance at Jake.

"What?" Jake asked.

"'Be back soon.' That's all you put?"

"What do ya want me to write? 'Off to rescue our kidnapped brother'?"

Huron shook his head and looked at Mari. "Honestly," he said, pointing a finger at Jake, "I don't know how he manages to make the grades he does."

Mari scratched his head.

"Never mind," Huron muttered.

"Hey, if you think you can do better, I'll gladly get another piece of paper," Jake retorted.

"Aww, let's just get going," Huron said.

Tails came up to him, whining. Huron comforted him, whispering, "Stay here. Everything will be fine."

The wolf nodded and placed his paw on Huron's foot. Huron gave him a pat on the head.

"Sit. Good boy. Stay," Huron commanded as they hurried out the door.

Tails sat down and didn't move. At last, the boys walked downtown, stopped at the bank, and headed for the bus station. Jake purchased three tickets, and they waited for the bus to arrive. Half an hour later, they boarded a dilapidated vehicle that had clearly seen better days.

The driver eyed them suspiciously and asked, "Aren't you boys a little young to be traveling so far? These are one-way tickets, son."

"Oh, we're just bone dry here. We need a little adventure, right, guys?" Jake said smoothly. They nodded.

The bus driver sighed and said, "Whatever. Go on and sit down."

They were about to sit when the driver spoke again. "Hey, hold on. What is that?" he asked. He was pointing at the handle of Aloha's sword.

"Oh, this?" Huron said, pulling on the handle. "It's a plastic sword for our cousin. It's his birthday in a couple of days."

"But I thought you said you were just on for an adventure?"

"Sir, while we like to be colorful, do you really think our parents would allow such a thing," Jake said in his most responsible—and lecturing—tone. "Why, I'll bet little Trevor will light up when he sees this present. He's into those *Teenage Mutant Ninja Turtles* right now. And, of course, I can't wait to have a heaping helping of Aunt Lottie's famous German potato salad."

"Hey, I didn't ask for your life story. This ain't *Cheers*. It's a bus. Now take a seat!"

"Yes, sir." Jake saluted him.

The driver rolled his eyes. He'd forgotten all about their one-way tickets. Mari gritted his teeth, completely unaware of it. He thought of Aloha bound in those rawhide strips. He must feel so alone and scared, he thought. He felt Aloha's fear coursing through his body, tightening his muscles. We're coming, Aloha. Mari did not realize he was glaring until Huron asked in a whisper if he was trying to pick a fight with the misfit with the Mohawk in the seat across the aisle. Apparently, the young man had thought them engaged in a staring contest. He blinked, glancing up in a disoriented fashion. Mohawk kid put on a smug face. Mari smiled, easily aware that this was no tough guy. The older kid grinned back.

Thirty hours later, they arrived in a blur of traffic and skyscrapers after miles of small towns, farms, and sunny skies. The bus eventually cleared the city and, much to their surprise, they were dropped off in some backwoods sub-suburban town that they couldn't even find on the map. Jake and Huron had no idea these buses ran route to such places, but it was an eerie feeling getting off in the middle of nowhere with only the sound of the wind. Mari felt like they had entered a modern-day western. Jake bought a Wisconsin map and a Minnesota map from the gas station in this rustic tourist trap, which didn't seem to attract any tourists. Maybe it just wasn't the season.

"Mari, why are you so quiet?" Huron asked.

"Yeah," Jake chimed in. "When Aloha's around, you never shut up."

"Oh, come now. That was just rude," Mari chided.

"You're right. I'm sorry."

"Humph. You don't sound sorry to me, buster." He put a hand on his hip and glared at Jake.

"Really, I am sorry. Truly sorry." He looked panicked then began to grin.

Huron laughed when they made up with a hug. This was the mood they started down the road with, heading toward the interstate. Jake, however, did not want to hitchhike and decided to find back roads out of the state instead. Huron turned to him.

"Hey, I thought your plan was to bus us to Minnesota? So why are we stuck here in Wisconsin?"

"Uh, well, I thought it would be more interesting this way, I guess."

"You are an idiot," Huron retorted.

"Correction: I am an idiot on an adventure."

"Moron."

"Correction: I am a moron on a mission. Who also happens to be short on cash. I still have a little bit of money, but I didn't have enough for the mileage to Minnesota."

"Excuses, excuses," Mari teased.

"Okay, okay, just shut up," Jake said.

At first they just followed the same endless street out of town for miles. They took a short break around two o'clock. Jake rummaged through his pack. He had brought a small lunch cooler from home with some sandwiches inside, and they ate ravenously. That night, they settled down in the trees and bushes bordering a farmer's field. Mari tried to sleep, but his eyes kept opening. He got up when he heard thunder. Rain soon followed. Mari climbed up a nearby hill to watch the storm. The confusion in the sky reflected his conflicted feelings. What am I doing on this journey, he thought. He was grateful for the chance to help Aloha, but he still didn't understand how he'd changed into a human in the first place. He surmised that he was allowed to be one for this rescue mission because Aloha needed him.

Certainly, he was happy to be aiding his friend, but he was concerned about the upcoming battle. He focused on the storm again. Maybe I will be able to fight for Aloha after all. Rain drenched him, but he didn't care. A feeling of power surged through him, and he felt one with the lightning. Every fiber of his being crashed with the thunder. The hair on his arms stood up, electrified. The clouds shook down drops of water as he stared up, enthralled. Cold streams ran through his hair, thrilling and chilling his tender skin. The water drops collected in tiny pools on his skin, on the ground, all over the place. His eyes glittered with the reflection of the tense lightning. Each time the already dissipated lightning's sound erupted in his ears, his grin widened.

Startled, he realized that he was happy. The rain, the cold wind, and the thunder were responsible. It was similar to swimming through the ocean at top speed. The rain on his skin reminded him of the salt on his dolphin skin as he skimmed the ocean for fun. It was over too soon. Soaked, he returned to the bushes beside Jake and Huron. He hunkered down with them on the least muddy piece of ground he could find.

As he lay down, his body reminded him that he had never been so sore. Jake and Huron were only slightly sore because they were used to being active on land, but Mari had been complaining from after the first hour of walking. His feet hurt so badly that they itched and felt heavy. His leg muscles were currently in spasms. Groaning, he huddled up and fell asleep. Hours later, he got up and crawled out of the bushes, walking away into the field and up the hill where he sat the night before. The day was dark with storm clouds. It might as well be dusk, he thought. He sat down and looked upward. Thunder crashed and lightning flashed, and soon an abysmal feeling had welled up inside of him.

Aloha's face flashed before him. He knew Aloha was brave, but he was by himself in a dark, dark cave, bound up in painful leather strips and victim to an unseen enemy. Mari pictured his lonely visage and promised with even greater determination that he would not let him down, that he would save him and bring him home.

The others woke up some time around noon. They ate some peanut butter and crackers that were among the meager provisions in Jake's pack and were off again. Man, Mari thought in agony, I should really start doing calisthenics or something. This time they made it through four hours of Wisconsin scenery before they took their first rest. So far, they'd walked about eight miles of glorious and painful terrain. The forests were lovely, and the shrubbery was restless with the scurrying of life. Mari enjoyed these sounds. It made him feel connected to the throngs of life radiating from the center of earth's throbbing heart. Huron kept teasing Mari for lagging behind, and Jake suggested numerous times that he try working out on a treadmill.

"Oh yeah," Mari said between pants, glaring at him. "Well why don't you try swimming like a dolphin? You humans think you're so smart."

Jake sucked in a deep breath and said, "I'm sorry."

"No, you're right. I shouldn't be so cranky. I guess I'm still having some trouble with this walking thing."

"Hey, you're doing great."

"Yeah, you've only been human for a few days now," Huron added.

Mari thanked them for their understanding. At five-thirty, they sat down to lunch. It was a light meal, for they were running out of rations. They rested until six and headed out again. It was a couple of days before they ended up in the middle of the state and found themselves at a diner just off of an interstate. They entered, having by now run out of food, cold and wet from the rain. The warmth was pleasing and comforting to their chilled skin, and the lack of a crowd made everything feel more intimate. There were a few scattered souls in the tattered blue booths, but no one paid them any mind. They were all too busy glowering at a man sitting in a booth near the window who would not shut up. He was prattling on loudly and detaining the waitress with boring details about his life that no one cared about. Goodness, Jake thought, I hope I never do that.

Jake ordered some delicious and greasy appetizers for them with part of his remaining twenty-five dollars. After the trio exited the diner, they crossed to the back of the poorly lit parking lot. Jake began trying the door handles on cars.

"Jake, what are you doing?" Huron asked, appalled.

"Trying to find us a ride to hitch," he grunted, pulling on the tailgate of a huge Chevy Blazer with Ohio plates.

Jake suddenly pulled them down to the right side of the Blazer. A man in a dark suit walked up. Mari recognized him as the one who had chatted almost nonstop in the midst of the solemn quietude of the diner.

"This guy said he was gonna go to Minnesota. I remember that," Jake whispered.

The man unlocked the Blazer but had apparently forgotten something in the diner. He turned around and jogged off, luck being on their side, and they climbed into the back, using his suitcases and blankets to conceal themselves.

They awoke the next morning to a sizzling sound. Jake sat up slowly, looking around cautiously and rubbing his head. Huron suddenly began to laugh. Jake and Mari gazed at him with quizzical expressions.

With a sly smile, he informed them, "This guy is frying eggs on his engine."

They exploded with laughter. It was a good thing they were in the very back of the guy's Blazer; otherwise, he might have heard. Upon peering very carefully out the window, they discovered that the SUV was parked along a highway. There was a sign that said they were six miles from Taylor Falls. Huron got very excited all of a sudden. Jake joined him in his eagerness.

"We're in Minnesota," Huron burst out.

"Yeah, and we need to get out of this Blazer," Jake said, "because we're not too far from the area that creature came from."

"Wait, how do you know we're even in Minnesota?" Mari asked, though he sensed a strong presence here and was calm all of a sudden. Aloha's face jabbed at his mind.

"We used to live around here," Huron reminded.

"Oh, right." He could hardly contain his excitement. Aloha, Mari thought, hold on. With that, the group slipped out of the side of the Blazer while their chauffeur was distracted by an annoyed police officer.

While the driver calmly explained that he was just eating breakfast, which wasn't a crime—"This is still a free country, after all, isn't it?"—they hurried into the forest.

Huron transformed into a wolf and said, "Jake, you and Mari go to the cliff next to the dirt hill, and I'll meet you there. I'll see if I can pick up Aloha's scent."

"You got it, li'l bro," Jake said as his brother dashed off.

"Where are we meeting him?" Mari asked.

"It's a spot not far from where we used to live. It was Huron's special place."

"You mean like that hill where Aloha goes to think?"

"Exactly," Jake said.

Razzmatazz the Goblin

Aloha was bleeding. This leather was cutting into him. Blood trickled down his wrists and snaked down his hands, dripping off of his fingertips. Everything else felt numb except for one annoying sensation. He had to go to the bathroom. Frustrated, he looked around for a way to solve this problem but could find none. Just great, he thought. Motion in the shadows drew his attention. Brightness suddenly flared in his face. He had been here for ages and hadn't seen any light at all. That might have been because he had been in and out of consciousness. A funny, crackling laugh broke the silence. From behind the light stepped a ridiculous looking creature that almost made Aloha laugh in return. The creature was about his height and lime-green in color. Its ears were giant and rimmed with blue. Little ruffs of hair stuck out from the insides of the ears. A tuft of turquoise hair topped its forehead. Its neck was also covered with a shaggy mane of turquoise hair.

The monster's snout was similar to the muzzle of a cat, but it had two elongated nostrils similar to a dragon. It was wearing a magenta shirt and ragged maroon shorts with a yellow patch on them. Fanning out behind it was a plumed pink tail. The creature's hands and feet were furnished with yellow claws. Aloha thought that it looked almost like a child's stuffed toy. The coldness in its laughs, however, put aside any sense of amusement he could glean from the sight.

"Welcome, human," the creature whispered.

Aloha shuddered at the thing's rasping, malicious voice. "W-who are you?" he stammered.

The monster bowed gracefully and replied, "I am Razzmatazz."

"What exactly are you, Razzmatazz?"

He snarled and shouted, "I'm a goblin."

Aloha shrank back. Razzmatazz continued his tirade. "Everyone thinks we're cute and fluffy, but then they find out how vicious we can be. I have plans for you, Aloha."

"How do you know my name?"

"Everyone knows the tide swooner."

"Really? 'Cause I thought I was the most un-famous ten-year-old that ever—"

"Silence," he interrupted. "I need your powers, young one."

Aloha whimpered a bit at Razzmatazz's nasty tone. Razz bared his teeth at the boy and revealed vicious fangs. Aloha gulped.

Razzmatazz rubbed his hands together and went on. "You are my ticket to glory and power. As tide swooner, you must know of that fiend, Barrett."

Aloha clenched his teeth and nodded when the goblin looked at him.

"Ah, so you also bear a grudge against him. I am going to defeat him and become the ultimate evil power. I shall rule the evil creatures of the world brutally." Razzmatazz waited for him to ask why, but Aloha looked away and slumped his shoulders. The goblin went on, "Do you have any idea how embarrassing it is to be evil when you look like this? Hmmm? That hellion Barrett has all the respect, while we goblins get nothing. All the other monsters and demons laugh at us, say we're cute. We may not be as ferocious and ugly as folklore has portrayed us, but we are not cute!

"That pompous Barrett once said that we goblins were nothing more than Halloween costumes. But the worst insult of all, the one I hate the most, is that we goblins look like adorable little children's toys. Can you imagine the shame of such a remark?"

Aloha shook his head.

"But with your power, I shall wreak my revenge."

"It's not my power," Aloha muttered.

"What did you say?" Razzmatazz growled at him.

Aloha closed his eyes tightly and hunched his shoulders together, shaking. "I said it's not my power."

"What are you talking about?" bellowed Razz.

"The power belongs to God. He merely uses me as a dwelling for his power."

Such a look of wonder came over Razzmatazz's face when he said this. For a moment, his whole face was transformed into a gentle mask, and he really did look cuddly. Then he let out a long, sarcastic cackle. Somehow, this got to Aloha more than anything else. He started, painfully aware of his need to go to the bathroom. He groaned.

"Why are you carrying on like that?" Razzmatazz questioned. His eyes narrowed.

"Please don't get mad. But I really, really gotta go, if ya know what I mean," Aloha told him as timidly as he could.

"Oh, for the love of…Get up, come on." Razzmatazz pulled the boy up and shoved him forward. Aloha couldn't feel his legs, and his steps were slightly above the quality of a stagger. His goblin companion pushed him into another tunnel near an underground river.

"Here," he told the boy, "go here."

"I can't move my hands."

With a snarl he untied Aloha's hands, watching his every move. Aloha turned his back to Razz and relieved himself. When he finished, he turned back to the goblin, who grabbed his bloody wrists and squeezed. The boy howled. The pain had already been substantial. Now it was unbearable. Razzmatazz pulled him to the river, thrust his hands into the water up to the wrists, and began using one clawed hand to rinse the blood off. The whole time Aloha whined in agony. Finished, he pulled the young tide swooner's hands out of the water and began wrapping his wrists with cotton gauze. Aloha tried to get the water in the stream to rise, hoping to use it for his defense by attacking and flooding the goblin with it, but to his surprise, the power did not come. Nothing flowed through him.

Razzmatazz bound his charge once more with the leather strips. Aloha couldn't fight back. He was too weak and in too much pain. He was led back to the cavern. Razzmatazz departed, and Aloha lay down, surrendering to the situation. He rolled onto his side and stretched his arms above his head. He turned his head into his shoulder and sobbed, muffling the sound with his shirt. Jake and Huron were never going to find him. They should have been here by now, he thought. I'll bet they're having fun with that new kid. He gritted his teeth. The *thock, thock, thock* of approaching footsteps surprised him out of his anger.

"Human, I have brought you sustenance. I suggest you eat and drink, because it's all you'll have for a while," said Razzmatazz.

Aloha couldn't see the smirk on Razz's face, but he could hear it. He ate a few peanut butter and banana sandwiches and drank six goblets of water. Despite his being a goblin, Razz was a good host, for an evil villain who'd abducted him from his home.

Mari bolted upright, slammed into wakefulness, and nearly knocked himself out in the process. His chest hurt. Man, what happened? Surveying his surroundings, he found they were camped near a creek. Behind them was a dirt hill that bordered a huge bluff. Jake was asleep on the ground beside him. Huron was not back yet. Mari's heart pounded. He looked at the sky and saw that it was early morning. He had a strange feeling that the hushed sunlight was calling him out into the open.

He got up, following the winding creek for a few yards. The compulsion stopped. He sighed with frustration. He began having serious doubts about their rescue efforts. He and Jake were clueless. They hadn't seen Huron since he'd told them to meet him here. That was over twelve hours ago. What do we do now, Mari wondered. Something was brewing inside him. His eyes grew large. An urge to cry out seized him violently. I, he thought, throat constricted, want to speak, I need to. Who do I need to speak to? A tiny whisper in his heart said, "I'm here."

Who? Mari thought.

"Pray," instructed the still, small voice.

It sounded almost like a thought-voice of his, except he knew this one was not his own. For the first time ever, he sank to his knees and bowed his head. It was the Creator commanding him. I've never heard His voice before, Mari thought.

"God? I've felt your presence near me many times, but I have never called to you by name. I need to know what to do. Please, save my friend." Amen, Mari thought.

"Wait," the Creator told him.

"Wait?" he responded. "How can I wait?"

"Everything in my time. Wait."

"I'll try."

He sat down on a log with his legs dangling in the creek. Mari noticed Aloha's backpack sitting beside him. Must've grabbed it without realizing it, he thought. Aloha's sword was tied to the back of it. His eyes fell upon it, and he decided to pull the dagger out and study it. This time, he felt no sense of foreboding as he opened the pack. Peering inside, he spotted an envelope that appeared to be sealed. What's this? He grabbed it and turned it over. It was addressed to Christina and Roger Christoph. I wonder if those are his parents, he thought. He wondered why Aloha had never opened it. Something about that letter seemed urgent, pressing. He reached to tear it open and realized that it only appeared to be sealed. Did that mean Aloha had read it? He decided to look it over anyway.

As he read, his hands shook and tears slipped from his eyes. The letter dropped from his hand as he finished, blinking for several moments. Slowly, his eyes moved down to the ground where the letter lay. I better pick that up, he realized. He snatched it up and scanned it again. Well, his question had been answered. Aloha couldn't have read it. Mari slid the paper back into the envelope and stuffed it into the backpack. He cringed, having no idea what to do with the knowledge he had just gained, As he turned to head back to camp, a flash of movement stopped him. Huron approached in wolf form.

"Mari. Guess what," he cried.

"What?"

"I've picked up Aloha's scent."

Mari whooped. "Let's go wake up Jake."

Wolf-Huron nodded, tongue lolling from his mouth.

It was midmorning, though Aloha remained unaware of it. He shivered in the cold and damp. For the moment, he was alone. Razzmatazz was busy in the underground stream. Aloha lay on the floor of the cave, staring into the darkness. As he watched, the glare of a lamp flooded his surroundings. It lit everything up so brightly, it hurt his eyes. His heart pounded, and he curled up into a fetal position. He raised his arms over his head as best he could to shield himself and squeezed his eyes shut against the light. His whole body quaked uncontrollably.

Wolf-Huron entered along with Jake and Mari. "Here he is," said Huron.

Aloha opened his eyes at the sound of Huron's voice. His heart rate slowed, though he was still shaking. His face brightened when he saw Jake and Wolf-Huron then fell when he beheld the strange boy holding the lamp. Jake and Huron glowed with relief as they eyed him. Mari ran over and embraced him gingerly.

Aloha cringed and snapped, "Hey. Who're you?"

Mari stepped back, confused. Sudden understanding dawned in his eyes. "Oh. Aloha, it's me, Mari."

"Mari?" Aloha's jaw dropped. He looked over at Jake and Huron. "What gives?" He narrowed his eyes at the stranger. "You can't be Mari. He's a dolphin."

Jake interjected, "It really is him. Huron and I watched him change into a human."

"I don't believe it. If you're really Mari, prove it. Tell me something only he and I would know."

"Your real name is Brian. I nicknamed you Aloha because of your shorts."

Aloha gaped. "I guess it really is you." He looked hard at Mari and nodded. "Yeah, you have the same eyes."

"We should really get out of here," Mari told him.

"Get me out of these ropes, then. I can't believe you decided to go human."

"Just temporarily," Mari replied. His voice had an odd ring to it, reverberating with dishonesty.

He's hiding something, but what, Aloha wondered. "Nice look on you, man."

"Thanks."

Mari cut Aloha's hands free with the dagger and handed him his sword. Light glinted off the end of Mari's dagger. "What the—" Mari began.

He cried out as the dagger let out a stream of gleaming light and became a shining sword the same length as Aloha's. Mari gazed at it with awe, and an understanding seemed to come to him. A roar of sound came from the corridor behind them.

"Oh no. He's coming back," Aloha whispered.

"Who?" Jake asked.

"The monster that took him," Huron said.

Razzmatazz entered the cavern. His eyes lit with malicious comprehension. A sneer appeared on his lips. "So your friends have come to rescue you after all. We'll just see about that."

Jake and Huron burst into laughter. Mari's eyes widened at the sight of the goblin. Aloha clamped his hand on Mari's in a vice grip.

"Are you serious? This is the big, bad kidnapper? He's so adorable," Jake cooed. "Hey, little fella, wanna come home with me? I'll let you be my pet."

The goblin snarled, exposing his pointy fangs. Jake started. He and Huron took a step back. Huron uttered a warning growl and bared his teeth at the goblin. Razzmatazz rushed Jake and knocked him down. Huron leapt on the creature, snapping his jaws at the back of the goblin's head. Razz howled, whipped his head around, and latched onto Huron's muzzle. Huron yelped and stood up on his hind legs. He thrashed his head from side to side. Razz fell off and tumbled over. The goblin recovered his balance and darted at Aloha. Jake got up and stood in front of Mari and Aloha.

"Run," he yelled at them.

Mari grabbed Aloha's hand and pulled him along. Huron ran up between Mari and Jake and flashed his teeth at Razzmatazz. The goblin easily dodged him and shoved Jake aside. Pivoting with eerie grace, Razz charged Aloha. Mari stepped in front of Aloha and raised his sword. The goblin rolled his eyes. He raced forward. Mari swung his sword and missed.

"You won't stop me," Razz cried, sidestepping Mari.

The goblin pounced on Aloha. Aloha managed to cut Razz's arm with his sword, but it wasn't a deep wound. Razzmatazz pushed him to the ground and seized his wrists. "I will not be denied your power," he shouted.

"Ah," Aloha shrieked as Razz squeezed his injured wrists.

"Aloha!"

"Mari, help."

The goblin uttered a snarky laugh. "What's he gonna do? He couldn't even hit me with that sword."

Mari ran forward and swiped at the creature's legs. His sword connected and sliced into thick green fur. Blood oozed out from the wounds. Razz let out a strangled cry and let go of Aloha.

"You," was all Mari could utter.

Shaking with rage, he grabbed the goblin by the throat, attempting to subdue him with the point of his blade. Razzmatazz scratched at him, spitting and hissing like a cat and cutting him across the cheek. Mari turned his head as the creature prepared to leap at him. Aloha rushed forward and sliced the goblin across the knees. He brayed in pain. Mari plunged his sword into Razz's heart. Razz fell to the ground, wheezing. Mari yanked his sword out of the goblin's chest. He shot up with deadly swiftness and knocked the sword out of Mari's hand. It clanged as it bounced along the floor and ricocheted off a stalagmite. Mari toppled over when Razz collided with him.

"Mari," Aloha screamed. *Father, I need your strength. Help me to defeat this villain*, he prayed.

Aloha's weakness was gone. A surge of energy went through him. He felt every hair on his body stand up, compelled by the energy. Electric warmth flowed out through every pore in his skin. His mind was invaded by the relief and wholeness of that energy. His entire being began to glow, for the power could no longer be hidden within. His body was not able to contain it.

At last he glowered at the creature. "Enough," he commanded.

Aloha shut his eyes, and they watched as light rose from within him and filled the room. It was a cross of pure energy. Aloha motioned his head at the monster, and the light swung forward and cut the goblin in half, obliterating Razzmatazz. When the remains were completely dissolved, the light disappeared. With the energy gone, Aloha was hollowed out. He slumped to the ground. Mari caught him as Huron transformed into a human.

Mari looked down at Aloha. "That was some battle. You all right, Aloha?"

He was shaken but replied, "I'm fine, really."

A hand touched Aloha's shoulder, and he looked up to see Jake and Huron.

"You two okay?" Jake asked.

Aloha nodded. Mari said, "I got a few scratches, but I'll live."

"Good. Can we get out of here now? This place is really starting to freak me out," Jake said.

"Yeah, let's go," Aloha agreed.

Once they were outside the cave, he stopped them. He examined them for a moment. Finally, he lowered his eyes to the ground and whispered, "Thanks for rescuing me."

The boys said not a word as they embraced him. Jake was the first to speak.

"Let's rest when we get to the camp, shall we?"

The others agreed. They hiked back to the campsite where they had left the rest of their things. After their rest, Jake suggested that he and Huron walk to Taylor Falls and get some cheap burgers from a fast food joint.

"Jake, who serves burgers at this time in the morning?" Huron asked.

"Most fast food joints quit serving breakfast at ten-thirty. It's ten o'clock now, but by the time we make it to Taylor Falls, it'll be around eleven. So let's get moving," Jake responded.

"Great idea, I'm starving," Aloha said.

"Me too," Mari added.

"We'll be back by noon," Jake promised.

"All right, that gives me a chance to take a nap," Aloha announced as they started to walk off. Jake flashed a thumbs-up at him without turning around.

Aloha stretched out on the ground, his eyes heavy. Mari said something that he couldn't make out. Soon, he was asleep. Mari glanced over at Aloha's book bag. He could feel the pressing weight of the letter contained within. *I'll tell him when he wakes up*, he decided. Meanwhile, he lay in the dirt beside Aloha. He spaced out for nearly an hour. His mind focused sharply when he heard Aloha sit up. Mari turned to look at him.

Aloha shook his head. "I can't stay asleep."

"I know how you feel," Mari said. He grabbed Aloha's old backpack.

Aloha narrowed his eyes. He blanched. "Why'd you bring that?"

"I needed a bag to carry stuff in. But I found something inside that you need to see."

"What's that?" His lips trembled. He watched Mari put his hand inside the bag and bring something out.

"Here," Mari said, holding out the envelope, "you need to read this."

"Huh? What is this?"

"A letter to your parents."

"What do you mean?" Aloha inquired.

"I found this on the way here. I figured it might be important, so I read it. Go on, have a look."

"I never even realized I had this." Aloha began to read the letter aloud:

"Mr. and Mrs. Christoph,

I have searched twelve years now for your lost son and have failed to find him. However, recent information strongly suggests that your son was ditched in Sarasota, Florida by his abductors. Witnesses place a little boy all alone at Turtle Beach about eight years ago. The description of the boy was similar to the age-enhanced computer rendering of your son. The last place they remembered seeing him was the Turtle Beach parking lot. I regret to inform you that I can no longer be of any help to aid you in finding your son, Mari, but I hope and pray that he is returned safely to you and your husband.

Wishing you luck,

Sherman Davis, P.I."

All the color drained out of Aloha's face as he spoke. He turned to Mari, gawking. "This means…"

"Yeah," Mari replied, "we're brothers."

"I don't know how to react."

"Neither do I."

Shocked, Aloha lapsed into silence. Mari gave him some space. He understood how Aloha felt. Jake and Huron arrived just before noon. The subdued reaction to the long awaited burgers puzzled Jake.

"What gives? I thought you guys were starving. What'd we miss?" Jake asked.

"I found out that Mari is actually supposed to be human. And what's more, he's my brother."

Jake groaned. "It's too early for any more weirdness."

Huron smacked his forehead then dropped his hand, placing it over his heart. "I am so confused," he murmured.

"What's to be confused about, Huron? This simply means that there will not be as many leftovers from now on," Jake grumbled.

"Listen," Aloha interrupted, "Mari found a letter I must have picked up the day my parents died. I never realized it was even in my book bag, but Mari found it."

"So don't keep us in suspense, dude. Hand it over," Jake said.

Aloha handed him the letter, and he and Huron read it over. When they finished, their eyebrows rose dramatically. Aloha stifled the urge to grin.

"Okay, wait. If he's your brother, how'd he become a dolphin?" Huron inquired.

All eyes fell on Mari. He shrugged. "I don't have an answer for that."

"Let's just eat before the food gets cold," Aloha suggested.

As they ate the tasty burgers, they discussed how to get home.

"We're gonna have to fly home," Aloha said simply.

"Won't someone see us?" Huron asked.

"Not if we fly at night and if we fly high above the clouds," Aloha said.

"So you can help us all fly?" Jake questioned.

Aloha nodded. "Ready?" he asked them.

"Most definitely," Jake said.

"Absolutely," Huron stated.

Aloha touched their foreheads and said, "Believe and jump."

Jake and Huron jumped and were delighted when they rose up into the air.

Mari jumped. To his dismay, he fell right back down. "Why can't I fly?"

Aloha came over to him and touched his forehead. Then he said, "Believe and jump, Mari."

Mari jumped again and felt weightless as he floated through the air. He laughed. It certainly was easier to maneuver through the sky as a human than it was as a dolphin. Aloha called them all back down.

Jake looked at him. "How come you never taught us to fly before?"

"I hadn't figured it out yet. Mari could fly as a dolphin when I told him to jump into the air and follow me because he was an animal, and I can exert a small influence on animals. But none of you could fly without my touch and command, because you're humans. You require my touch to dim your analytical tendencies and close down the disbelieving part of the human mind. Then you can be imaginative easier and follow the same command that allows animals to fly."

"How did you figure all this out?" Jake asked.

"I had been thinking about it awhile, and I remembered something my mother did the night her spirit came to me to tell me about Shakoda. I had no idea what it meant at the time, but when she touched my forehead and said to believe and to jump, shortly after I was able to control my ability to fly."

"Oh," Jake said.

"How come you could fly before that?" Mari inquired.

"I think it was her spirit that carried me those times."

"Oh, yeah, I saw our dad lift you up that night you and I were flying," Mari said.

"Really?" Aloha said, eyes wide.

"Yes."

"Cool," he exclaimed.

"How did you know for sure that what she did for you would work on us?" Huron asked.

"I wasn't entirely sure, but it seemed like too much of a coincidence to write off," Aloha replied, shrugging.

"Enough, enough. You're making me dizzy," Jake complained.

"All right. We should get going," Aloha said.

"I thought we weren't going to fly until it got dark?" Mari asked.

"Yeah, but we can still walk for a while," Aloha explained.

Mari groaned.

Homecoming

When they had arrived safely back in Siesta Key, they detoured to Turtle Beach, and Aloha noticed that Mari was frowning.

"What is it?" he asked.

"It still bothers me that I don't know how I became a dolphin."

"We can explain that," said the voice of the maiden.

Their parents' appeared in spirit before them. Their mother wrapped her arms around Mari, holding him tight. He clung to her as their father hugged the three of them.

"Mari, we are so proud of you. We've wanted to explain all this for so long, but certain rules about what can be revealed to the living prevented it," she said.

Their dad smiled. "I know you always saw us helping and guiding Aloha, but we've been here for you, too, even when you felt alone. I caught you when The Goyle dropped you. And you saw me watching over the two of you."

"I can't believe you're my dad too," Mari stammered.

His mom added, "Mari, let me explain how you became a dolphin. You see, we were on vacation down here when I was pregnant with Aloha. On a morning walk, I met a young boy—you, at age four—who said he was all alone and wished nothing more than to become a dolphin. Well, nothing like this had ever been requested of me. I prayed and asked for guidance. The Lord said He had a special plan for you and allowed me to grant your wish, and I found a family for you that I thought would love and take care of you. But they didn't, did they?"

"How come you didn't know who I was?" he asked.

"When you were only four months old, you were taken by a neighbor couple. See, I had to go to the hospital because my mother was sick, and your father had to work. I asked the neighbors to babysit you. This lady and her husband had watched you often, so I had no reason to distrust them. While I was gone, they took you, and when I came home, the three of you were gone. So, when I saw you four years later, I did not recognize you."

"It was you," Mari said weakly. The world was spinning away. He fell to his knees—and remembered.

The two people who had taken him were a couple of yuppies. By the age of two, he knew something was wrong with them, but as time went by, he had no choice but to think they were indeed his parents. He spent almost four years with them; and in that time, he could not figure out why he did not connect with them. Mari felt bad about this. He really wanted to make them happy and proud, but everything he did seemed to upset them. As awkward as it was between them, it got even worse when other people were around.

One day, Mari was playing with his blocks. He was building a ladder to the moon for his little dinosaur figures. This way, they wouldn't have to be extinct. He heard a car door slam outside. If he'd been paying attention, he'd have run and hide. However, he was focused on his task.

"There. Now you guys can be safe when the meteor hits."

From the kitchen came the jarring sound of Mom's voice. "Mari, come see your Aunt Dorothy."

Mari cringed. He hated Aunt Dorothy. She reeked of a sickly sweet odor that made him want to vomit. She also had a frightening face. It was always crinkled up, but her skin drooped and sagged. But worst of all were her eyes. She had beautiful, light brown eyes, but in them was a severe, heated look. He always sensed that she was just dying to pick a fight and barely able to restrain herself. His mother found him. Saying not a word, she grabbed his arm and hauled him into the kitchen. Mari began to cry.

"Mari, Aunt Dorothy has come to see you. Why do you always look so scared? You stop being such a rude little boy."

Aunt Dorothy grabbed him and smothered him with a hug. "How's my big nephew?" Her breath smelled like coconuts and rotten fruit. Her eyes lit with an eagerness that Mari did not understand, but he recognized the need for caution. He began crying again. "This boy is such a sulk. Really, Gina, you must get him checked out."

"I will. Mari, go play."

He left them. Later that day, after his aunt had gone, he was in the living room reading his favorite picture book. His father and mother walked through the hall. He heard his dad say, "Why does he have his nose in that book all the time? There's something not right about that kid."

Mari hid his tears in the book. It hurt when they said things like this, which they did a lot. Everything he did embarrassed them. There was a knock at the front door. Father answered it.

"Oh hey, guys."

Great, their friends are here, he thought. Panicked, he tried to hide. Their friends caught him trying to slip behind the couch.

"What's he doing, trying to hide?" The man who had asked, Sam, shook his head.

His wife, Sharon, said, "He's got such sad eyes. He's kind of a creepy kid."

As soon as Sam and Sharon went home, Father turned to Mother. "Even our friends don't like him. This was a mistake."

"I know. The kid is a constant disappointment. But what can we do? We can't take him back."

"I have a plan. Let's go on vacation."

"What?"

He smirked. "Trust me."

They went out for a while, leaving him home alone. He did not mind. He was used to it. Mari was in his room when they got home. Mother came in, smiling gaily. She set a suitcase down beside him.

"Guess what, Mari? We're going on vacation."

Mari remained silent.

"We're going to Florida. Aren't you excited?"

"Sure." This was all he said.

She watched as he quietly went about picking out the playthings he wanted to take and pointing at the clothes he wanted her to pack. Such an inscrutable child, she thought. The plane trip didn't scare him in the least. He remained uncommunicative as he read his picture book. It seemed the safest thing to do. Once they landed in Bradenton, they drove to Sarasota. Father stopped at a place called Lorelia's Café, and they had lunch. They left the car in the parking lot when they finished and went for a walk. Father fished in his pocket for his small area map.

"Mari, this map says there's a beach nearby."

"Yeah?" Mari asked shyly.

"Yes. It's called Turtle Beach. Would you like to go see it?"

"Yeah."

They walked to the parking lot of Turtle Beach. His father stopped. A thought seemed to occur to him. "Mari, would you like a sno-cone? I'm sure they have them somewhere around here."

"Sure, Daddy."

"Wait right here. Your mother and I will get you one. Don't move, okay?"

"Oh. Okay."

Mari turned his back on them and looked at a hill just in front of him. It blocked the view of the ocean. Hey, he thought, they didn't ask what flavor I wanted. A few people walked by as Mari waited. He looked away from them. Ten minutes later, Mari began to cry. Now he knew for sure. Mother and Father aren't coming back, he realized. What's wrong with me? Why don't they want me? He sat down on one of the yellow-orange parking dividers. A shadow fell over him, and he started as he beheld the woman standing before him.

"Why are you crying?" she asked.

"I'm all alone. I hate this place. I want to be something else."

"What do you mean?"

"I wish I could be a dolphin and swim in the sea."

"I can help you with that, but are you sure you don't want me to find your family?"

"They don't want me. They left me here."

"What if I take you in?" the pregnant woman asked.

He looked at her, full of distrust. "No."

The woman frowned for a moment. She paused, lost in thought. At last, she said that she knew of a dolphin pod in the area that would likely take good care of him. "Are you sure you want to become a dolphin?"

"Yes. Please turn me into a dolphin."

She took him into the ocean and prayed. Then she touched his forehead with salt from the water. "Be bonded with the ocean," she said, and he was transformed.

He was too young to remember this when introduced to the dolphin pod, nor did he remember their reactions to him. Mari was amazed at the knowledge flooding through him.

"Mari, are you all right?" Aloha asked.

He shared his memories with them.

"How could anyone not love you?" their mom wondered.

"You are one of the finest kids alive," their dad agreed.

"Thanks, you guys." He was bursting with happiness at this praise, which he had never received from the dolphins. "I just have one question. Do either of you know why Shakoda kept calling me a guardian?"

The maiden smiled. Her husband looked at her and said, "You want to field this one, honey?"

"Sure. The villains you encountered knew who you really were. They knew you were the protector of my heir, the tide swooner.

Because fate worked out the way it did, you became your brother's guardian. This must have been part of the mysterious plan for you all along."

Mari sulked. Aloha glanced at him, saying nothing.

"What's wrong?" his mother asked.

"Why wasn't I chosen as tide swooner," Mari demanded. He folded his arms against his chest.

"My dear Mari, you had the most important job of all," she said.

"I did?"

"Yes. A big brother's job is to protect his younger brother. And you have done that."

Mari smiled evenly. "I guess I have."

"That's right," Aloha added, slinging an arm over Mari's shoulders.

Jake and Huron, who had been watching in awkward silence, turned to leave.

"Come here, boys," called Aloha and Mari's dad.

They hurried over, and both parents said, "Thank you for being there for our sons. We shall look at you as our adoptive sons, since your parents are going to be taking care of both of ours now."

They grinned and thanked the spirits. The two spirits waved at all of them before they vanished. The boys, now a full-fledged family, watched them fade then turned toward home. Aloha told Mari that he would help convince his adoptive parents to adopt him, too.

"I have a plan," Jake announced.

"No offense, bro, but your plan to integrate me into the family sucked," Aloha said.

"True," he agreed, "but if we disguise Mari well enough…"

"Jake," Huron groaned.

"Okay, okay. We'll try it your way." He flashed a thumbs-up.

They hurried home. Mari's stomach felt like a washcloth being wrung out. Their mother and father were on the porch swing. Mari's future parents looked up expectantly.

"Where on earth have you boys been for the past week?" Marisol demanded.

"And what's with that note? 'Be back soon.' I can tell Jake wrote that," Jimmy said, casting a disapproving stare at each of them.

The boys exchanged looks, equally amazed that the police had not been called and, in fact, their parents seemed to be expecting them to come home on their own, uninjured and in no danger. At last, Aloha spoke.

"Uh, Mom, Dad, this is Mari."

"Hello, Mari," greeted Marisol. "As you may have already figured out, our sons are in a lot of trouble. You may want to excuse us." Jimmy nodded curtly at Mari.

"No, he can't go. This is partly about him," Aloha said.

Marisol and Jimmy stared at him. Jimmy tapped his finger on the swing's armrest. Aloha looked down at his feet. "Young man, I don't like to be kept waiting," Jimmy warned.

"We've been on an adventure," Jake burst out, "and it was so cool! We went back to Minnesota to battle a goblin."

Jimmy's eyes went wide. His wife sighed. "Even if we believed this outlandish story, why would you boys need to travel to Minnesota and battle a goblin?" Marisol asked.

"Because the goblin kidnapped Aloha," Huron interjected.

"Yeah, duh, Mom," Jake added.

She glowered at them. "And so, even if this were true, instead of telling your father and I and having us drive you or get you plane tickets, you what? Walked?"

Huron and Jake were silent. Jimmy snapped, "What'd you do, buy bus tickets?"

Blushing, Jake nodded.

Ignoring this exchange, Marisol turned to Aloha. "Were you, as these two claim, abducted by a goblin?"

Aloha nodded and added, "But when you put it that way, it does sound far-fetched."

"You think?" Jimmy asked sarcastically.

Jake looked at his dad and said, "And you didn't think to try and find us or call the cops?"

"Young man," roared Jimmy, "by the time the three of you are finished being grounded, you're gonna have hair growing out of your ears."

"Let's just put aside this kidnapping business for a second," Marisol said. "Someone tell me how this boy fits into all this," she beseeched, pointing at Mari.

"Okay, so," Aloha intervened, "we recently found out that Mari—well, he used to be a dolphin."

"Wait. You expect us to believe that the last two years you've had a dolphin as a friend?" Jimmy said and rolled his eyes. Marisol shook her head in disbelief.

"Um, yeah. Anyway, see this goblin with a weird name abducted me, and they came to rescue me, and Mari turned into a human to save me. In my backpack, he found a note to my parents from a private detective saying that my brother, Mari, who had been kidnapped, was alive and in this area to the best of his knowledge. My mom turned him into a dolphin without recognizing him because he'd been taken when he was so young. He knows the truth now and must remain human. So now, he needs a home," Aloha finished breathlessly.

"Oh, you have a note proving he's your brother? Well that solves everything, now doesn't it? May we see this mysterious note?" Jimmy quizzed, an acerbic smile pasted on his face.

Aloha nodded to Mari. "Hand it over, Mari."

Mari dug out the letter and handed it to Jimmy. He read it, and his sardonic expression softened. He handed it to Marisol. She read it over, the color draining from her face. "Jimmy, this looks legitimate."

They exchanged looks; and for one horrible moment, Mari thought they would ask how his mother could have been able to turn him into a dolphin, but they didn't. Marisol seemed to believe them, for she had tears in her eyes. Jimmy seemed won over as well.

At last, she said, "I'm so glad you found each other. You two belong together, and we're going to make sure that happens."

"Thank you," Mari said.

Jimmy turned to Aloha and chided, "Next time, tell the truth. You don't need to make up a cock and bull story about him being a dolphin or about how you were abducted by a goblin. And Jake, you should know better than to go off on a quest to find his brother by yourself. You boys need to come to us for help. Understand?"

"Yes, Dad," Jake whispered.

Jimmy looked pointedly at Aloha, who nodded sheepishly. Then he glanced at Mari and said, "Welcome to the family, son."

Mari grinned. "Thanks, Dad."

"Just so we're clear: you boys *are* grounded for the next month," Marisol chimed in.

"Well, that seems fair enough," Jake replied.

Jimmy and Marisol busted up laughing. Things were going smoothly. That is, until Huron said, "And you wanted to disguise him."

Jake blushed, and Jimmy said, "Well, at least that was better than your last idea."

"I know; that's what I told them." He grinned with pride.

"I think this calls for a celebration," Marisol said. When she had everyone's attention, she looked at Jimmy and asked, "How should we commemorate this occasion?"

He thought for a moment. "Why don't we go for a carriage ride tonight?"

"Oh yeah, we've never done the tour of Siesta Key before, have we?" Marisol replied.

Aloha's heart leapt into his throat. For just a second, he was back in the parking lot of Oceanrise again, carrying his suitcase to the van. He came back to the present. Mari watched him, concerned, until a magnificent grin broke out onto his face. "Oh, can we, please? I always wanted to do that."

"All right, it's decided then," Jimmy said.

That evening, the six of them got into the carriage. Two white horses pulled the carriage along the beaches and through Sarasota. They whinnied as their breath wafted out into the chilly night. Aloha oohed and aahed at the glistening white sand that magically captured the moonlight. The midnight blue sea sparkled as the stars glittered above. The carriage headed back up the beach and onto the road. Jake, Huron, and Mari had their sights fixed on the buildings. In the shadows, the houses, restaurants, and bungalows appeared to be a magical kingdom. Mari could almost picture Razzmatazz skulking about the buildings and alleyways, ready for mischief. He shuddered.

Aloha discovered this view as the horses clomped down Midnight Pass. His eyes dashed along the streets and sidewalks, between the palm trees, and into the neatly manicured yards. There were decorative fences and trellises and flowers galore. It's all so perfect, he thought. When they got home, they topped off the celebration with key lime pie.

"Wow," Mari said through a mouthful of pie, "this is really good."

Marisol beamed. "Glad you like it, Mari. I made it myself."

"It's fantastic," he added.

Jimmy leaned close to him and whispered in his ear, "Don't listen to her. She bought this at the store. She just takes advantage of anyone who doesn't know."

"What're you telling him, Jimmy?" Marisol demanded.

"Nothing, sweetheart."

"Knowing Dad, he's filling his head with useless information," Jake quipped.

"Like father, like son, wouldn't you say?" Jimmy asked Mari.

Mari laughed. "So that's where he gets it."

"Now do you see why I have a hard time punishing you boys? How can I punish you when I know my husband's up to his own mischief," Marisol said.

Jimmy balked. Jake pointed at him, laughed, and said, "See, now you know how I feel."

Jimmy favored him with a stern gaze. "Watch it, smart Alec." He elbowed Mari. "You see what I have to put up with? I get no respect."

Mari nodded. Jimmy brought a forkful of pie toward his mouth. At the last second, the pie slid off the fork and plopped onto the kitchen floor. Heedless of everyone's stare, Jimmy took his finger and swiped up most of the pie, then licked his finger clean. Everyone gaped.

Jimmy looked about. "What?"

"That's so gross," Marisol complained.

"I didn't see no devil touch it," Jimmy replied, winking at Mari.

For a moment, Aloha and Mari glanced at each other, an eerie thought crossing their minds: *If only you knew, Dad.* In spite of the chill that went through him, Mari smiled at Jimmy's statement. Marisol grabbed his shoulder and bent down, whispering, "He's actually worse than Jake. I'm not kidding."

Mari laughed.

"Is she feeding you misinformation? Whatever she said, it's a lie. She does that," Jimmy teased.

Marisol hit him gently on the head with a dishtowel. "Jimmy, stop setting a bad example. Remember how you made those kids in the grocery store cry last week?"

"They were crying because they were terrified of you."

"Yeah, because you told them that I turn into a witch every Halloween and eat children."

"Well, I have yet to see any evidence against it," he explained.

Marisol rolled her eyes. "Oh well. Just another day in paradise, right, Mari?"

"Sounds like it," he agreed.

They spent the rest of the night bantering back and forth. *So this is what it's like being part of a family,* Mari thought, *what fun.* Late that evening, after everyone had gone to bed, he awakened and left the room he now shared with Jake, walking out into the night. He thought he finally understood why Aloha always wandered out here when troubled. Now all the hard and yet joyous truths he had discovered swirled around in his mind as he tried to integrate them into his knowledge.

"It's the perfect spot to think, isn't it?" Mari turned toward his brother's voice. Aloha put a hand on his shoulder.

"Yeah, it is."

"We're real brothers now, Mari."

"Yes."

Aloha smiled. "I always wished for a brother like you. And all this time you've been right here."

Mari nodded. "I am glad we found each other."

"I believe things are going to be all right for us now."

"Me too," he said. "Aloha, I was just wondering. What were our parents like?"

"Hmmm. They were both very kind and caring. Stern but loving."

"Where are we from?"

"We were from Warwick, Rhode Island. Dad was the captain of a cruise liner, so he was gone most of the summer, which meant we took our trips right before school started. And Mom was a plumber. Oh, and she had a pilot's license."

"Did you ever get to fly with her?"

"Once. It was fun."

Mari smiled. They walked home in silence. The roar of the ocean waves spoke volumes for them. As they entered the house, Mari whispered, "They're not coming back, are they?"

Aloha shook his head. "I don't think whatever rules govern that sort of thing allow them to."

"They'll always be up there, looking out for us."

He nodded. Mari snuck back to his room. Although he was saddened, he had nothing but happy dreams. Aloha had gone back bed too. For a long time, he lay in bed, lost in the past. Restlessness overtook him, and he got up again. He slipped into Jake and Mari's room and watched Mari sleep for a minute. Mari was snoring loudly, and Aloha stifled a giggle. He heard a creak behind him.

Entering the room, Jake said, "Just great. I get the one that snores. Figures that Huron gets the quiet, cuddly one. Although, at least he doesn't drool like you do, Aloha."

He smirked. "Yeah, but I feel sorrier for Mari. You talk in your sleep."

"I do? Am I coherent?"

"Not a chance."

"Rats. Well, I'm turning in, bro, so scram, will ya?"

Aloha waved as he left, adding, "Have fun with Captain Snore-face."

Jake put a hand over his mouth to cover a laugh. "Goodnight, Pillow-wetter," he teased.

Aloha hesitated when he got to the door of his room. He dropped his hand from the knob and crept downstairs and out the sliding door. There was somewhere he needed to go. It took hours flying at his top speed, but just before daybreak, Aloha made it to the house where he'd lived with his parents in Rhode Island. He snuck through the bushes and cautiously pushed open the picket-fence gate. As he slunk through the open gate, he looked around. Whoever lived here now had painted the house. It was hard to tell what color it was in the dimly approaching morning light, but it was darker than the modest tan it had been. He jerked his head about, taking in the lawn. Even that had changed. Where his mother's garden had been there was now a sandbox and a jungle gym. The big oak that his tire swing had hung from had been cut down. Not even the stump remained. This is not my home anymore, he reminded himself.

Aloha turned to leave and scanned the neighborhood. One of these houses harbored two kidnappers, he thought, balling his hands into fists. He glared at the dark houses before walking away. Once he was out of the neighborhood, he took to the sky and flew to a nearby bluff overlooking Greenwich Bay. The vastness meandering before him was overwhelming. His heart raced until he remembered that he wasn't alone and that Mari would be there to help him out, as he had done from the time they'd met.

A smile emerged on his face. As the sun rose, glimmering upon the water, a voice came from within the light rays basking him.

"Well done, faithful servant. Your family is whole."

Elation and warmth pulsed through him. "Father, is that you?"

"I speak; I am."

"I will listen," Aloha said. He fell to his knees, bowing his head.

"You are the last of the tide swooners. You must stop Barrett, but it will not be his last appearance. One is coming who is stronger than you. He shall be the one to finally put an end to Barrett."

"What do you mean? If another is coming, how can I be the last tide swooner?"

"This one will have even greater power than the tide swooner. He shall have a new title. I have given him full and final authority."

"What will his title be?"

"It is not for you to know."

"But if he's the one who will finally defeat Barrett, why send me? Why should I fight him at all?"

The voice grew stern, responding, "What is your mission?"

"To defeat Barrett," Aloha answered, shrinking down even more.

"And who is your master?"

"You, oh God, and your son, the Lamb."

"Then why do you question my authority?"

Aloha gulped and blushed. "Because I want to understand."

The sternness went out of the voice. Aloha heard a thunderous chuckle. *I hope that's a good sign,* he thought.

"Evil," explained the Father, "must be dealt with in every generation. But the world shall have a brief reprieve. That is what you are fighting for. It's what you are sacrificing for, my servant."

"Father, why does evil exist?"

"Everyone must choose between freedom and slavery. Humans must learn what freedom truly is and what bondage really means. Humanity has yet to figure out which is for the better. But one day, they will see the truth displayed before their eyes, and all evil will be vanquished."

"Why not now?"

"Patience, little one. It is not finished."

"What isn't finished?"

"My plan is yet incomplete."

"Why can't you finish it now?"

"Dear child of the herd, you are a sheep in a pen. You see only a small portion of what is before you. But I see the whole of creation. I know all things. Your story in the thick of things is but one patch of the quilt. I see how everyone's heartical journey connects. You only see a snapshot. As my loyal servant, you must accept your destiny and face Barrett."

"Why'd you create evil, anyway?" Aloha covered his mouth, instantly regretting what he'd just asked.

"It was not my creation. It was the result of a choice made by my creations. It remains a choice."

"I guess I understand," Aloha said. He scratched his head, lost in thought. He wasn't even aware that the voice had finished speaking.

Kiro

One Year Later

The sun rose, climbing ever higher in the sky and lighting up the world with its burning glow. Aloha and Mari got up about eight o'clock with Huron. Huron decided to walk down to the village that was about two miles from their home, but Aloha fancied a stroll along the beach. Mari decided to visit Eden. His wonder and excitement at finally being able to step over the land and explore still awed him, even after a year. He could see the greens springing up in front of him, ferns and tropical plants and palm trees, a deliriously alluring overgrowth. Somehow it looked even better from up close than it had from the sea.

    Mari stretched out on the beach and daydreamed about what life would have been like if he and Aloha had never been separated and their parents were still alive. He suspected Aloha would still be tide swooner, but even if he were still Aloha's guardian, he would be content. The only downside is that we wouldn't have Jake and Huron as brothers, but maybe we would have met them during one of our vacations here. A scenario sprang to mind. He saw Aloha in their hometown of Warwick, Rhode Island. Aloha—or Brian, as he would be called—would probably take after their mom. He'd end up being a plumber or a tradesman of some sort. Mari pictured the two of them working together in their plumber's uniforms and smiled. Then he envisioned himself taking after their dad onboard the cruise liner that he captained. Mari would learn from him and become his assistant.

Another image of Aloha and their mom on a small plane came to him. That's right, she had a pilot's license. I bet Aloha would have one too, he thought. He could see himself and his dad accompanying them on flights in a small yellow and white plane. And then there would be their vacations to Florida. He and Aloha would both be excellent surfers, of course. They would meet Jake and Huron out on the waves and become fast friends. The two would be excited as they listened to Aloha and Mari's adventures on the ocean and aboard the cruise ship. Then they would be bowled over when they discovered Aloha and Mari's mother was the Maiden of the Sea and would ask to meet her. It would be so wonderful. But it's a foolish dream, he realized, because we can't go back.

He got up and seated himself upon a sea-facing rock. A voice hailed him. Mari turned to see Alpha dolphin staring at him. This surprised him because he had warned Alpha that this area was dangerous.

"What are you doing here? Shouldn't you be with your friend, that Aloha kid?"

Mari read his intentions wrong. He glared back. "Always the same response from you: disdain. For your information, Aloha is the tide swooner. He's our mother's heir."

Alpha looked only mildly interested. "And your point is?"

It felt good to get the truth out there, and now he was going to hammer it home. "You rejected me, but I am her son, the maiden's firstborn. How do you feel now that you know the truth?"

"I feel nothing."

Mari balked. "All this time I was her own son. How dare you continue to disrespect me."

"But apparently not her favored son, since you are only a guardian. It would appear that your destiny has been stolen from you."

Hurt all over again, Mari yelled, "Why do you hate me so much? Everyone hated me, but you most of all. Why?"

"I don't hate you," Alpha said, showing no emotion.

"Then why do you never care about anything I do? Why was I never good enough?"

"I've always felt your difference. You're not part of my world or my family. You never were. It was not intended that you should be. That is the way it has always been."

"That's no reason to be so cold."

He turned to Mari. "I did not want to get attached."

"What?" Something in his eyes got to Mari.

"You were always special. But I knew one day you'd be taken from us to go back to wherever you were from. How could I let my pod know that my heart left with you? I simply vowed not to let it happen."

Mari gasped. Alpha was admitting his love for Mari. But a thought struck him. "That doesn't make any sense. If that's how you felt, why did you try to brand me?"

"If I had truly intended to, that blow would have made a mark. I had to push you away. Your destiny was not with us, no matter how much I wished it."

All along, he thought, I was wrong.

"You think I hated you. No. Once I found out that you were her son, it cut me deeply. I was jealous."

Mari remembered Alpha's soft and noble speech at his mother's funeral. In that moment, he realized that Alpha had cherished his mother as queen. He must feel the same about me, too, Mari thought. Alpha began to swim away.

"Alpha," Mari called.

"What now?"

"Thank you."

Alpha nodded curtly, but a smile was on his face. "I'd have found you this morning, no matter where you traveled, you know," he called as he left. Mari wiped a tear from his eye.

Mom had a special saying for moments like these. Mari started, recalling what Aloha had told him about the sad moments being beautiful because they were part of the heartical. He smiled. I think Mom was right, he decided. It is beautiful in its way. Heartical is the patchwork quilt of life on earth.

Aloha heard the sound of soft laughter from behind him. He turned to see a girl with short, light brown hair and green eyes running toward him. He waved at her, happy to have company. She was about his height and, man, was she fast. She sped over to him and held out her hand, grinning. He shook her hand.

"Hi, I'm Kiro. I just moved here. Who're you?" she asked, unable to contain her delight.

"Hi, Kiro. I'm Brian, but everyone calls me Aloha."

"Cool. Wanna be friends, Aloha?" Kiro said, bouncing from one foot to the other.

"Sure. How old are you? I'm eleven," Aloha told her.

"I'm eleven too. Hey, did you see that kid with weird purple hair? I saw him on my way over here. He was headed toward the village."

Aloha blinked. He'd never known many girls, so he didn't know whether they were all this strangely energetic or just some of them. Kiro's overeager attitude was a test of endurance for him. "I think that would be Huron, my older brother. He's thirteen," Aloha explained.

"Really? Wow, he's shorter than you," she exclaimed.

"Yeah. I know. But he's really cool," Aloha told her with pride.

"Awesome."

They spent the morning chasing each other around and battling with swords. It turned out that Kiro didn't have a sword, but she had a wooden staff with a nail in the end which was supposed to be a spear. *He's good with that sword, and he's fast, but maybe I can use the length of my spear to my advantage,* she thought. Kiro blocked his next blow. She shifted the spear so that it was straight in front of her. Aloha was forced to jump back.

Every time he closed in on her, she brought the spear forward so that he had to back up. She's keeping me at a distance, he realized. Clever. Aloha responded by trying to cut the spear and break it, but just before he could strike it with his sword, she would jerk it up. Kiro was baiting him, drawing him close and forcing him back. I can't beat her, he thought.

"So where did you get that thing, anyway?" Aloha asked.

"My godfather made it for me," she told him.

"Really?"

"Yeah. After David made this spear for me, I went and ran into my friend, Nathan. And I showed him, and he was scared. Can you believe it? I mean, sure, his parents were right there, but they weren't scared. I was pretending to be an Indian. Let's just say after that, I never looked at Nathan the same way."

Aloha wondered how she had looked at this Nathan. Man, girls are so confusing, he thought. They continued their battle, resting between rounds. Kiro dodged his blows and struck with her spear. She kept the spear held high enough that the nail didn't accidentally hit Aloha. He had to admit that he was surprised that she could keep up with him. Even Huron couldn't keep up. The battle ended in a draw.

"Hey, Kiro?"

"Yeah?"

"How can you fight so well?" Aloha inquired.

"Oh, I don't know. I always used to pretend I was Robin Hood, so maybe that explains it." She shrugged and added, "It was the only time I ever voluntarily wore tights."

That doesn't really explain anything, he thought. It didn't matter. He found her peculiarities more and more appealing. This kid is interesting, she thought. He always looks perplexed. She appreciated how nice he was and enjoyed the challenge he provided her. His imagination also suited her. Most of the boys she'd known were boring and unimaginative. That wasn't to say they didn't use their imagination, but they were so cliché.

Everything they'd play was based on movies or TV. They did not have the creativity to come up with their own games or stories. But Aloha did. She could tell by the look on his face that he'd been making up a story to go along with their game. His eyes had been focused but also clouded with a daydreaming gaze.

"Kiro, you should come to my house," Aloha suggested. "You can meet my brothers."

"Brothers? You mean you have more than one?"

"Yep."

"That's so cool. I'm an only child," she told him.

"I used to be," he quipped.

Kiro scrunched up her face as she tried to read him but said nothing. They raced back to his house, matching each other's strides. Aloha was impressed that she was such a good runner. *He's so fast. He gets much faster, and he'll win,* she thought. Luckily, he was running his fastest, and she kept pace fairly well. As soon as they got to the house, Huron walked up.

"I thought you were going down to the village?" Aloha asked.

"I couldn't get near there with all the tourists," Huron explained, "so I came back."

"Oh. Hey, Huron, this is Kiro. She's the same age as me."

"Nice to meet you, Kiro. I like the spear," he complimented.

"Thanks. It's nice to meet you too. I saw you walking earlier."

"Yeah, I enjoy walking," Huron said.

"He's rather lackadaisical when walking, too," Aloha chimed in, "always ambling about."

"Stop teasing, Aloha. At least I don't meander around with a dazed expression on my face all the time," he countered, a sly smile on his face.

Kiro looked back and forth between the two as Aloha added, "You talking about Jake?"

Huron nodded, covering his mouth. "Good one, Aloha. So what do you like doing, Kiro?"

"I enjoy running," she replied.

"You must be good to keep up with Aloha. I saw you guys racing up here."

Kiro laughed as Huron smiled. They jolted when a car pulled into the driveway. It was Jake. He parked his car and got out. Spotting the three of them, he came over. At the same time, Mari returned from Eden.

"What've we got here?" Jake said with a smile.

"Jake, Kiro," Aloha introduced.

"Hey, little chick." Jake nodded at her.

"Hi," Kiro replied. "How old are you, Jake?"

"I'm eighteen. How old are you?"

"I'm eleven."

"Sweet."

Mari cleared his throat to get their attention and introduced himself. "I'm Mari, Aloha's older brother. Nice to meet you, Kiro," Mari said, holding out his hand.

Kiro shook his hand. "Wow, Aloha's got an awful lot of brothers."

"Yeah, guess he does," Mari agreed.

Once everyone got acquainted, Aloha suggested that they teach Kiro how to surf. Mari jumped at the chance. Aloha and Huron had taught him to swim and to surf after they got back from Minnesota, and he'd fallen in love with it. Kiro also enjoyed it, but it took her an entire month to be able to stay on the board. Every time she fell off or wiped out, she laughed and tried again. Aloha enjoyed watching her take things in stride. *I think we're gonna be good friends,* he noted.

One morning, he took her out near Eden to practice, though he steered her away from dangerous waters. Hours were spent in the chilly wind as the two surfed. The sun was setting in the sky when they decided to call it a day. He signaled to Kiro. She nodded in return. Aloha started to look away, but out of the corner of his eye, he saw her pitch forward, off-balanced. Her board slid into the water nose first. Kiro's body hit the surface viciously.

Aghast, he flew into the air. He pushed his hands up, and the water rose up, lifting Kiro to his level. He grabbed her and flew to Eden's nearby shore. Aloha set her down. She was unconscious. He put his hand under her nostrils to make sure she was still breathing. Hot breath warmed his hand. Relieved, he waited for a few moments, and her eyes opened halfway.

"Aloha, did you save me?"

"Yes." Aloha blushed.

"How? What happened?"

"You crashed into the water pretty hard, so I used my power to help me move you to shore."

"Huh? What power?" Kiro pried.

"I'll explain after you get some rest."

"Oh. Okay, I guess." She closed her eyes and was out a minute later.

Aloha moved his hands over her forehead, using the same healing massage he'd applied to Mari after he was injured during their treasure hunt. When Kiro awakened, he was busy fixing the sky with a pondering gaze. She sat up.

"What are you doing?" she queried.

"Looking for my parents," he said quietly.

"Huh? Aren't they back home?"

He flushed again and looked down. "Sort of."

"What do you mean?"

"They're my adoptive parents, and Jake and Huron are my adoptive brothers. Mari is my natural brother. Our real parents died."

"What happened to them?" she whispered.

"I don't want to talk about it right now." He avoided her gaze.

"Okay. But I'm still wondering what you mean by that whole power thing."

He ran a hand through his hair and sighed. "My mother was destined to be protector of the sea. She had certain powers. When she died, I inherited them, and with them, the responsibility of protecting the ocean and its creatures. I bear the title known of tide swooner. And that's pretty much it."

"Wow. So what can you do?"

"I can manipulate the ocean waters or any water. I can fly and make others fly. I can also breathe underwater unassisted for a short period of time. And I can heal people."

"Cool," Kiro said.

"Yeah, it's all right, but it's also work. And I've got an important mission to fulfill, too."

"You have duties? Like what," she grilled.

"Well, nightly, I have to fly across the world and make sure no one is endangering any of the ocean animals or polluting and destroying the ecosystem. I have a pod of orcas who are my envoys of the sea, who act as my eyes and ears in case any danger comes along. There is a whole network my mother set up to get this information to me. But most importantly, I have to find and defeat the source of all evil."

"The source of evil? You mean it actually has a source?" Kiro asked.

"Yes," Aloha responded. "His name is Barrett. Once I take care of him, there will be no more evil threats to this world for a while, except for those initiated by man. But a time will come when one greater than I will arrive. He will stop Barrett for good."

"I don't understand."

"Welcome to my world," he joked.

"You won't go after him without me, will you? Please let me come with you," she requested. "I'd love to see you defeat this Barrett dude."

Aloha looked chagrined. "Uh, I dunno. I don't want you to be in any danger."

"Psh, come on. I could help you. You know I'm good with a sword."

"That's true," he said. "The thing is, I don't have any idea where Barrett is. I'm not sure if I will find him or if he will find me, but I know at some point we will meet. It's fate."

"Heavy," she said.

"Yeah," Aloha agreed.

Kiro laid her head on his shoulder, startling him. "It's all right. You'll knock that creep into oblivion."

Aloha smiled. Her confidence was contagious. "You think so?"

"Definitely."

Trauma

Summer, Three Years Later

Another summer, Kiro thought happily. She blushed when she realized that she would be spending more time with Aloha, and she had no idea why. Aloha and I will be alone? She gasped, her heart pounding very hard all of a sudden. Wait, Huron and Mari will be there, too. That relieved and disappointed her. She sat down on the curb, her hands draped between her legs. She didn't want to go home. Lately, there had been a lot of tension in her house, and she didn't know where it was coming from. Pressure rose in her chest and behind her eyes. She let out a strangled breath. With one hand, she rubbed at her temple. She was so oblivious to her surroundings that she did not hear Aloha walk up.

"Kiro," he said. "Smile, it's not that bad." When she didn't respond, he leaned over her and tilted his head quizzically and asked, "Kiro? Are you sleeping or something?"

She jumped, looking around in alarm. Her alert posture unnerved Aloha.

"Huh? Aloha. Hi," she whispered languidly, wiping her eyes. It was a reflex action.

"Hello."

"What do you want?" she asked. Her face turned bright red.

"Well, I thought we'd go swimming. I'll be your companion if you like of me," he said elegantly, making her laugh.

Instantly, all her sadness melted away.

"Is that a yes?"

"Yeah, affirmative," she told him with a nod.

Aloha took her hand and led her to the beach. As they walked toward the water, he glanced at her, concerned. *I wonder what she was doing when I came up.* Her blank expression and rigid posture had reminded him of his parents' faces after they were hit by the car. And then, when he had spoken to her and she hadn't responded, he saw his parents strapped down on the stretchers. Now, he drifted back in time, lost in unwanted memories of that day.

Kiro frowned. Aloha had been awfully quiet. A coil of unease unraveled in her stomach. She said his name, and this time he was despondent. *This must be what he felt like when he saw me spacing out,* she realized. His eyes grew wide, and his skin paled. Frightened, she waved her hand in front of his eyes. They didn't follow the movement. Something was wrong with him. They had just reached the fringe of the water-licked beach, and she reached out and stopped him from walking straight into the ocean. Aloha sank to his knees, and she dropped down beside him.

"Aloha?"

He turned his head toward her, eyes vacant.

"What's wrong?" she asked.

He blinked. For a moment there was only the sound of the waves to break the silence. At last he said, "When you were spacing out on the curb, it reminded me of the day my parents died."

Kiro held her breath, her chest falling flat in shock. Her lips parted a second later, and she began sucking in small breaths as Aloha spoke.

"You remember that day when we were surfing, and I told you I was adopted?"

"Yeah."

"I wasn't ready to tell you about my parents. I guess I need to talk about it, though. It's been a while since I've thought about it."

"Okay," she whispered

"We were staying at Oceanrise on vacation. It happened the morning we were leaving for home. Dad and I headed into the office to return the condo key. Mom was sorting through the mail. Before we went in, Dad suddenly pulled his wristband off and pressed it into my hand. He said to take care of it for him. Anyway, when we came out of the office, Mom got out of the van. She started to say something to Dad, and he told me to stay put then went to her. They were speaking in low voices about something.

"Suddenly, this c-c-ar jumped the curb and was flying at them. They saw it coming, but there was no time for them to move. And it sideswiped them, crushing them against the front of the van."

Aloha shivered, remembering how he'd fallen to his knees, the thud of his backpack landing beside him. He had not seen the wind pry loose the envelope in his mom's hand. He had not watched the letter float and twirl its way down and under the van, moving like a feather as it made its descent to the small puddle of water next to the curb in front of him. But he had stared blankly at it for a moment then he reached out and grabbed it. Without realizing it, he had shoved the letter into his book bag, out of sight and out of mind.

"A man coming out of the office behind me called the paramedics, and they showed up a few minutes later. A crowd gathered around the stretchers. During the commotion, I ducked into the bushes. Since the police hadn't arrived yet, the EMTs were busy trying to get the crowd to back up. While they were distracted, I slipped unnoticed through the crowd and made my way to my parents. At first, both of them had their eyes closed and all their features were slack. When I saw you spacing out, that's what it reminded me of, and—" He couldn't finish. He sobbed as he leaned against her, and she put her arms around him, cradling him, his head against her chest.

She didn't know what to say.

"I took their hands, Kiro. I took their hands, and they opened their eyes for a moment. I don't think anyone saw it, but my dad opened his mouth and told me that he'd, he'd never leave me. He touched the wristband he'd given me, *this* wristband," he said, holding up his arm and showing her. He continued, "Mom couldn't speak, but he did. I'll never forget it, either. I don't know how he got those words out. His mouth was bleeding, struggling so badly to move. And sometimes I dream about the moment after he spoke, when they both went limp and died, and I wake up about to scream. I feel like I'm always stifling the tears and the screams," he cried, eyes widening.

He put his head on her shoulder, and she tightened her embrace as his sobs got the better of him again. Finally, he lifted his head and said softly, barely audible, "Do you know what the worst part is?"

"What's that?" she asked.

"The worst part is that they didn't make a sound, not one, when they were mashed up against the van. They opened their mouths, but nothing came out. That's the worst part somehow, that they never even screamed. They were robbed of words. I can't get that out of my mind. I feel like, like I should be shouting out for them."

Kiro remained speechless.

"I know it sounds childish, but sometimes I can't help thinking that they couldn't cry out because of me. Because I should have, should have—oh, I don't even know." He sat up beside her in the damp, cool sand.

"But you didn't do anything wrong."

Aloha could tell he was upsetting her and felt a pang of guilt. He started to get up.

She took him by the shoulders and held him down beside her. She protested, "You were only a little kid; there's nothing you could have done to help them. It was just a freak accident. If you want to blame somebody, blame the guy who hit them. He's responsible, not you. Tell me why you think you deserve to suffer for his mistake."

He sniffled, feeling free all of a sudden, free because he knew she was telling him the truth. "You're right," he said, "I'm sorry. I feel bad for putting all of this on you."

She shook her head. "I'm your friend," she told him with a sober smile.

"Kiro, you know, I love my family, but sometimes I wish things were different. I wish Mari and I were living with our real mom and dad. I mean, shouldn't I feel guilty for that? For wanting a different life?"

"You don't have to feel guilty. It's natural. They were your parents, after all. But things have worked out for you in the end."

"Yeah, I know," he said.

"One thing, though. Where was Mari when all off this happened? Why wasn't he there for you?"

"Well," he began and launched into the whole bizarre tale of how Mari was turned into a dolphin and how he ended up reclaiming his human birthright.

Kiro blinked uncertainly. Could he be lying to her? No. If Aloha said this had happened, then it must be true. After such a rough beginning, these two were lucky to be adopted into a loving family, she thought. "Wow. That is weird," she said at last.

"I know."

He sighed, and she said, "What is it?"

"The thing is, I can't feel their spirits anymore. Ever since Mari found out the truth, things have been different. I never wanted them to change. I always wanted to feel them near me."

"They told you they weren't allowed."

"So, just like we've been doing, we've got to find our own way," he said bitterly.

"Your own way, exactly."

"I'm tired of doing everything by myself," he complained.

"You're not alone," she pointed out.

"It sure feels that way sometimes."

"Aloha, they had to let you move on. And that's what you're doing. Sometimes it's hard to let go of the past. But you have to do it, or you'll never get anywhere. Think about what you've gained. You have Mari and Jake and Huron. Plus, if you had a different life, I wouldn't know you. I don't know about you, but I would feel lost without you. I mean, you're, like, my sunshine in this world, you know?" She blushed, and so did he.

Aloha caught a glimpse of sadness on her face. What's wrong, he wondered. "Gee, thanks. I would definitely not feel myself without all of you. You guys are my Mountain Dew."

She laughed, and the sound of it made him feel better. "Come on," he said, "Let's go for that swim now."

"Okay, but I have to warn you, if there are any sharks, I'm letting them eat you first," she teased.

"Hey," he shot back. "I thought you were my friend."

"I am. That way, you won't have to be grossed out by watching them eat me."

"How generous of you," he mumbled.

A week later, Aloha waved as he watched Kiro approach the porch. He was very excited because a new movie was out that he wanted to see about Shakespeare. Since entering high school, he and Kiro had gotten into Shakespeare's plays.

"Kiro," he exclaimed happily in his famous half-shout, half-laugh. "Guess what. I'm going to see that Shakespeare flick tonight. Want to go with me?"

She grinned. "I would, but I have to practice for track."

"But you're constantly practicing. You practice every day, plus I help you work on your speed after fencing. Besides, school's not for another three months. Give it a rest for today. Please," he pleaded, adamant that she should go with him.

She rolled her eyes. "I'm sorry, but my speed's been slipping a bit lately. I have to practice."

"But, but it's Shakespeare. You only, like, worship him."

"Yeah, but—hey, I do not. And you'd better stop. I'm not going."

He huffed impatiently. "All you ever think about is track, track, track," he grumbled.

"In case you hadn't noticed, I've been spending all my time with you," she responded indignantly.

"Oh, so now you're saying you don't want to hang out with me? Fine. Whatever."

"I'm not saying that. Why are you acting like this? We can just go tomorrow." What's his problem, she wondered.

"I don't even know why I bother hanging out with you," he muttered, instantly ashamed of such a hurtful lie.

"Well, if you want to go with someone so badly, then why don't you just take one of your admirers," she yelled just as he was about to apologize.

"Just forget it, okay. If you don't want to go with me, I'll go myself," he spat back.

"Why?" She snarled at him, antagonized into her own angry mood by his sharp comments. "I'm sure that Lindsay girl would *love* to go with you."

"What are you talking about? You know something, you've changed, Kiro, and I'm not so sure I like it." What is wrong with me, he thought.

"This isn't like you, Aloha, not at all." She was close to tears, and suddenly she thought, How dare he tell me I've changed. He's Mr. Popular all of a sudden, not me. She thought of how girls crowded around him in the halls at school and felt lost in a cloud of jealousy. Finally, she retorted, "I've changed? I'm not the one who has everyone noticing me but doesn't notice it. Sheesh, Aloha, all the girls at school do is babble about how cute you are and how they wish you'd go out with them. I mean, everyone is jealous of me for hanging around you, but none of them think I'm good enough to be *your* girlfriend."

"Well, you're not my girlfriend. I don't have a girlfriend, remember?"

"Well, who says I want to be," she snapped.

"Well, if you didn't, then why did you bring it up?"

"I didn't bring it up. I was trying to get you to understand how you've changed."

"All I understood from what you said is that everyone else has changed. I haven't. Why do you care anyway?"

"Because I...because you're my friend. I have to care about you, duh."

"But I thought you were mad at me?" he said, confused.

She rolled her eyes. "Ugh, you are the most unperceptive boy in the universe. This is stupid. I'm going home. Call me later, all right?"

"Fine, go home," he said, his voice rising. "How am I supposed to know what's wrong if you won't tell me?"

"You don't get it. It has nothing to do with you, anyway. I don't even know why I thought it did. I'm sorry for snapping at you, okay?"

He sighed, still angry but agreeing to consent. "Yeah. I'll call you later."

"Okay. Bye."

"Bye."

He watched her leave, still fuming. Man, this was the angriest and most annoyed he could ever recall being in his life. Aloha walked home, his temper gradually decreasing. When he got there, he sat on the porch with the portable phone, waiting for Kiro to call. He didn't know why, but he had a feeling that she would call before he could, and he wanted to be ready. While he waited, he went over and over their argument in his head. It almost seemed like Kiro had been trying to tell him something, but he couldn't figure out what. All he knew was that his heart had done a funny little leap when she'd said that no one thought she was good enough to be his girlfriend. That wasn't true. But he hadn't been able to say that. When she said that, his heart felt like it was wired to a car battery being jumped.

Meanwhile, Kiro hurried toward her house, but as soon as she was a good distance from Aloha, she slowed down. Her breath quickened and so did her pulse. She had a sudden feeling that she didn't want to go home. Cramps stabbed through her stomach. This has got to stop, she thought. She took deep breaths and waited until she was steady then got up and started for home again. When she got to her backyard, she sauntered to the kitchen door and opened it. What came out was an assaulting blast, a disgruntled, angry wave of noise lunging at her.

"Listen, I don't care whether you did or didn't. This is still my house, you know," her mother was screaming.

"Fine. Maybe I don't want to be in your house anymore," her father yelled.

"I certainly won't keep you," her mother shrieked.

"Fine," her father shouted as he walked past Kiro out the back door without noticing her.

Her mother turned, also oblivious, and stormed out of the room. She stalked toward the front door. Kiro knew her mother had left when she heard the front door slam shut. Shaking in disbelief, she grabbed the phone and dialed.

"Hello," came a slightly huffy response. Aloha had jumped when the phone rang, even though he'd expected it.

He's still mad, she thought and felt an insane urge to laugh. "Aloha, could you come over?"

"Kiro?" he said. Although he was still simmering over their fight earlier, something in her voice concerned him. "I'll be over in a few minutes," he told her.

"Thanks."

"Sure."

He hung up and ran as fast as he could to her house. Ten minutes later, he went around to the back door and, finding it wide open, rushed inside. Kiro was standing in the middle of the kitchen, the phone receiver still in her hand. She didn't appear to see him.

"Kiro? What's wrong?" he asked breathlessly.

"I think my parents are getting a divorce," she cried.

"Wha—what?" he stammered, taken aback. Whenever he'd been around, they had always seemed so loving to one another, like the perfect couple.

"I came home and saw them fighting. My dad said that he didn't want to be here, my mom said she didn't want him here, and then he left, and she took off. Neither of them even saw me. I'm scared, Aloha. What's going to happen to me?" She sobbed.

"Are you sure it wasn't just a bad fight?"

"Pretty sure. I've never seen either one of them that angry before."

Aloha panicked under the emotional weight of these revelations. What if she moves away, he thought, horrified. "I'm sorry, Kiro. I'm sorry we fought and that I was mad at you and that I was a jerk."

She hugged him and said, "Yeah, me too."

He was trying to cheer her up, but inside he felt a rush of anger: anger at her parents for doing this and anger at the world because he knew that no one could stop it. He assumed that things were probably better off in the long run, but why did it have to be so painful? All this rushed through his mind, and he was terrified that she might be taken away from him, and that wouldn't be for the better.

"Hey, it'll be okay. You'll see," he whispered, pulling her into his arms.

Test of Evil

A year had gone by since Kiro's parents signed the divorce papers. Her mother and father agreed that she should stay with in Siesta Key. She stared out her window at the predawn sky. Finally, she left the house. Shoving her hands in her pockets, she walked through the tall grass and shrubs onto Turtle Beach. Her father had called last night and said he wasn't going to be able to come see her today, even though it was her birthday. I hardly ever see him anymore, she thought. Doesn't he miss me at all? He'll probably send a card, at least. But I keep writing him, and he never writes me back. Can he really be that busy? Aloha would probably tell her that her dad was working a lot. Well, he did have to travel a lot for his job. I don't know, Kiro decided. Maybe if I visit Eden, I'll feel better. Something about the lush, ancient vegetation and thick underbrush made her heart soar.

She would watch the sun come up and transform the world while she waited for Aloha to wake up. They had plans to hang out later in the afternoon. Although Aloha wanted to spend time with Mari and Jake, who were back from college, he had agreed to spend some time with her too since it was her birthday.

Aloha heard the phone ringing and woke from his daze. He picked up the phone, feeling very edgy. I'm not in the mood for this, he thought. I just want to hang out with Jake and Mari.

"Hey, Kiro."

"Are you coming?"

"Yeah, yeah. Be there in five minutes, sheesh," Aloha told her and hung up.

He pulled his sandals out from under his bed and put them on. It hit him that instant how much he missed Jake and Mari. He was glad Mari was home and Jake was visiting for the summer. Sometimes he had Huron to hang out with, but Huron was usually busy. He had become quite popular in high school. He often invited Aloha and Kiro to come with him, but Aloha felt awkward because, being two years younger, he didn't have much common ground with Huron's friends. He had school friends of his own, but he mostly stuck with Kiro, because she was the only one he trusted with his secret about being the tide swooner. Besides, she also knew about his destiny with Barrett, something that still weighed on his mind.

Kiro was his best friend, and he enjoyed their time together. Yet, something felt incomplete without Jake and Mari living at home. Their parents were working a lot lately, so Aloha and Huron only saw them in the evenings. Sometimes in quiet moments such as these, Aloha felt very alone. He'd wind up thinking of his mother and father—his real mother and father—and it would leave him awash in sadness.

Don't think about it, he told himself. But lately, he couldn't get it off his mind. Something about the past still seemed up in the air, unresolved. Perhaps it was because he was still no closer to finding and defeating Barrett. And now he had to worry about Kiro. She missed her father lately. He dragged himself out of the room and down the stairs, trying to shut out this depression. He walked past the laundry room, grabbed a shirt from off the top of the dryer, and put it on.

Huron was in the kitchen. He looked up when Aloha entered. Frowning, he asked, "Are you all right? You look a little pale."

"I'm fine. Just tired."

"Oh. Off to meet Kiro? Keep her busy before her surprise party, okay?"

"Yeah. See you there later."

"Yep, see ya."

Aloha took off and walked down the beach past the hill and the boulder. There was the old rope bridge that stretched on in a not-quite-stable way and spanned the gap of a very small inlet. As he stared at the bridge, it lurched a little in the breeze and made the same creaky stretching sound as a rope swing swishing through the air.

Aloha started across the bridge. Already he could see Kiro sitting near a rock on the beach. But when he took in the scenery behind her, he gaped. The shadows in between the palms and ferns formed a looming shape like that of a dragon. One palm leaf slanted down into a pocket of dark space, and for just a moment, it seemed to be the slit of a revolting eye glaring back at him. He gulped. He'd never seen Eden in this light before. That's all it is, he thought, just the way the light is distributed. Still, he swallowed hard as he stepped off the bridge onto the beach. From the beach, the impression that the trees were looming was even greater. Instead of looking like a dragon, now the thick shadows looked like a mouth open wide. The trees reminded him of teeth jutting up, and the large, leafy plants between the trees coalesced into a giant tongue unrolling toward them. Aloha's mouth was dry as he forced himself to look at Kiro instead of behind her. He pasted a smile on his face and called to her. She turned to him, eyes shining with tears.

"Smile. It's not that bad."

She shook her head. "You wouldn't understand."

"Try me," he insisted with a sly look.

"It's just that my dad called, and he isn't coming to visit. I haven't seen him in months."

"Kiro, he's just busy."

"I know that." She sounded a little hurt.

"Look, I know what it's like not having your dad around when you need him, but you do have your mom."

Kiro rolled her eyes.

"And you know what else?"

"What?" she asked halfheartedly.

"You always have me," he said quietly.

"That's good to know."

Aloha was confused. How was he supposed to cheer her up before the surprise party when she was like this? *I know that I upset her, but I thought she wanted me here.* "Do you want me to leave? Because that's what it feels like."

A soft moan escaped her. "I'm sorry, but maybe you'd better go."

"All right. But it's not good to be alone when you're like this."

He turned to go, and she called his name, grabbing his hand. He careened toward her, only to meet her eyes dead-on. He saw the agony that was within and how much she needed him. She wanted him to stay, but she couldn't say the words.

"I just need some time to get out of this funk," she said.

Aloha smiled loosely. "It's okay. I'll come back for you in a while. You will at least let me walk you home, right?" *After all, I have to get her to the party,* he thought.

She nodded, too overcome to speak. Aloha waved. He hesitated when he got to the bridge and turned back. She really shouldn't be alone, he thought. Kiro had sat down again and wasn't looking at him. Aloha jerked his head up and looked behind her. He thought something had moved in the shadows beyond her. He waited and watched for a minute but saw nothing. Frowning, he crossed the bridge again. He was relieved when he was on the other side. He didn't look back.

Left alone, Kiro tried to make her mind blank, tried to remain indifferent to her pain, but the only thing she succeeded in was becoming drowsy. She leaned against the rock. As her eyes were closing, she thought she saw something slip into the trees. Whatever it was had glided back into the shadows. Her eyes widened and she gazed about, seeing nothing. Shrugging, she let her eyes close, sure that she ought to be headed home, then remembered that Aloha was supposed to come and take her back. She could nap while she waited.

When she fell asleep, a vision of a monstrous thing towering over her filled her head. It had serpent eyes and a ram's antlers, with a dragon's snout and big pointed teeth. It even had ghastly retractable claws on its gnarled and bumpy hands. It smiled coarsely down at her, its serpent's tongue flicking out between its gleaming teeth. She could feel its slithery grip on her and groaned as it jerked her into its arms. She felt it lift her up. Her eyes snapped open as it picked her up, and she discovered that she couldn't move. Rigid in its arms, she watched her surroundings blur by as she was carried deep into the dense vegetation.

I can't believe this is happening, she thought, dazed. Am I really awake? The beast set her down near a large rock resembling the one she had lain near previously. She had never been to this part of the island before. The plant life was so thick she and her friends hadn't been able to get through it. She shivered because this shadowy place was also colder. Her teeth began to chatter. The creature sat next to her and showered her with a slimy smile.

"I do apologize, young one," it told her. It opened its mouth, releasing billowing smoke and the horrid aroma of brimstone. Orange light came rushing up from the back of the creature's throat and past its immense fangs as it blew fire onto the rock, instantly warming her.

Kiro shrieked and tried to scoot away.

"Calm yourself," the creature said.

"Who are you?"

"My name, dear lady, is Barrett. I am your protector now. I will always care for you."

Suddenly, her eyes widened. She trembled. Barrett, she thought, her breath caught in her throat, this is the guy Aloha's looking for. "Barrett," she screeched.

"Ah, so you know of me?" inquired the fiend.

"You're the source of all evil," Kiro said with a gasp.

"Oh, young lady, you give me way too much credit. Evil is, was, and always will be. Every generation has its challenges."

"You are evil," she insisted.

Barrett's eyes glowed. "Humbug. Who says? I am a benevolent force for this world. My only desire is to help you, girl. I shall make it my life to serve you."

"No. I want to go home. Aloha is supposed to—"

He smiled. "To come get you? No, poor Kiro, he won't be here. You see, like everyone else, he has abandoned you. I am the only one who cares about you. You can be my friend and help me. If you want," he suggested, "we can even make them pay for hurting you."

No, he can't, she thought. Kiro could feel a weight drop inside her, crushing her under it. It was like she couldn't move, because it sucked all the energy out of her. "Aloha would never leave me here with you."

Barrett laughed. "Dear child, you are so clueless to the ways of the world and its inhabitants. Do you know that he forgot about you? He's off surfing with his brothers. He doesn't care about you any more than your pathetic father does."

Kiro jerked back. Maybe her dad didn't care about her. Otherwise, why was he always too busy for her? "Take that back. My dad does too love me," she protested.

"Does he? So that's why he is always ignoring you? Why do you think he doesn't bother to answer your letters? He does it because he can't stand to be near you."

At this she was puzzled. Why *did* her dad always disappoint her? Maybe he's right, she thought. Barrett could see her starting to crack open.

"In his eyes, just like everyone else's, you're worthless, a failure of a human being. They don't tell you this, but you're an embarrassment: very high maintenance and full of angst.

You annoy your so-called friends constantly. They laugh at you behind your back. But I see your worth. I understand how you ache inside, longing to be loved. I see the potential for great things in you. Your pain is an outrage and, together, we can make it your strength."

Everyone hates me? No, that can't be right, she thought. But if he's right about Dad, what about the others? She flashed back to her phone call to Aloha. He had sounded annoyed. Was it because of me, she wondered.

Barrett's eyes glowed. Yes, he thought, that's it, choose me.

He may be right about Dad, she decided, but that doesn't mean he's right about everything. She examined him with defiant eyes. "Take me home. I don't want anything to do with a liar like you."

"What have I said or implied that wasn't true? That your dad will never be proud of you? That Aloha will never see you as anything but a sidekick?"

She blushed at this but answered, "You said that together we could make my pain my strength, but only God can do that. And He does it by turning something bad into something good, not ruining what is good by using evil."

"You still think I'm evil? Please. I work for the Lord of whom you speak. You should look at those people who always hurt you and let you down, Kiro. They're the ones who are evil. Why else would they be so cruel?"

"But they're only human."

"But I'm not. And I can complete your emptiness."

"You can go fry yourself, for all I care." She cringed as soon as the words were out of her mouth.

To her surprise, Barrett laughed. "Good one. I shall do as you ask, barring the frying. I shall leave you alone for now." With that, he disappeared.

Kiro lay next to the rock. She could feel Barrett's gaze all around her and knew he had not gone far. She was resigned to the fact that there would be no escape. There never was. And once again, she'd have to face the darkness she'd been living with since her parents had split up.

"I just don't understand it," Aloha said aloud. "Kiro said she'd wait here for me."

He crossed the bridge and walked into Eden. Despite a cursory search, he could not find her. He pushed his hands through his hair. A strong sense of foreboding gnawed at his stomach. Frustrated, he turned and ran off to search the other places she frequented. He knew she liked a restaurant that was just a short walk from Turtle Beach, so he'd check there first.

Aloha scrambled up the steps to the wooden deck that was just outside Lorelia's Café. He held his breath, trying to shut out the memories that were crowding in. He had come here with his parents several times during their vacations to Siesta Key, and he could see them sitting at each of the tables he was dodging; and then he saw the cloudy sky, felt the rain coming down in cool droves as he waded through the crowd to get to the stretchers on which his parents lay dying. A new image formed: Kiro sitting beside him at one of the tables. *Not again. I will not lose her,* he told himself. He grabbed for the door handle, only to find it locked.

"Huh?"

He looked up to see a sign on the door bearing the word "Closed" on it. *Wow, they closed early today,* he thought. Aloha decided to see if she had gone home. He'd been there only half an hour ago helping get things ready for the party. He couldn't see her getting back there in the short time he'd been gone, but he raced to her house anyway. Her mother said she had not seen Kiro. Fortunately, she was too busy to notice the fear written on his face and wonder why he had asked. She responded absently and was heedless when he left. Once outside, Aloha hung his head then sprinted off to find Huron. Huron was at home with Mari. Aloha was pale and dripping with sweat by the time he got there.

"Aloha, what's wrong?" Mari asked.

"I can't find Kiro." He panted.

"What? Oh man, I hope she didn't go home," Huron replied, cringing.

"No. I just came from there. Her mom hasn't seen her either." He began to cough.

"Are you okay?" Mari said.

"I'm worried that something may have happened to her. She was supposed to meet me out by Eden. It's not like her to ditch me. Besides, I doubt she'd have left when she was waiting for me to take her home. I've searched everywhere I can think of, but I can't find her."

"Wait, I thought you were supposed to distract her while her mom set up?"

"She wanted some time alone, Mari."

"Oh. Was she all right?"

"I don't know. She was upset, like really missing her dad or something."

"Jake's here somewhere. We could go ask him for advice," Huron suggested, donning a thoughtful expression.

"Good idea," Aloha exclaimed.

They found Jake chilling on the porch swing.

"Aloha, what's up, li'l bro?" Jake asked.

"Kiro's missing. I was supposed to meet her, but she's gone."

"You sure she didn't go home?"

"Yeah. Her mom hasn't seen her. I've got an awful feeling about this. I just know something's happened to her." He ran his hands through his hair in a frenzied fashion.

Jake sighed and sat up in the swing. "Aloha, have faith. If you can't find her, then I know where we need to turn."

"You mean God?" Aloha asked.

"Exactly."

"I'll pray about it, but I'm still worried."

"Then it'll be okay. God helped us find you, and I'm sure He'll help us find Kiro."

"I hope so." *Father, help us find Kiro and get her home safely*, Aloha prayed.

"Come on, guys, let's go out to Eden and look for Kiro," Jake said.

A sharp bark came from behind them and stopped them in their tracks. Tails stood staring at them. Jake waved his arm and said, "All right, fine. Come on, boy."

Tails wagged his tail and followed. "He's getting a little too old for this," Huron muttered. Tails chuffed in offense. "Oh come on," Huron told him, "you're over seven." Tails growled as if to say, "Watch it, buddy." Huron rolled his eyes.

Once they arrived in Eden, Tails began sniffing for Kiro's scent. They followed him to a clearing a short ways from the beach. Suddenly, he backed up and started howling.

"What is it, boy?" Huron asked. Mari had the twisted urge to laugh. This reminded him of an episode of *Lassie*.

Tails howled again.

"Well?" Aloha said.

"He thinks something happened to her here, but her scent is gone."

"I don't know what to do," Aloha cried. "I don't even know where to start looking."

"Calm down," Huron told him.

"Calm down? Kiro's in danger. And I can't do anything because I have no direction. I feel like an endlessly spinning compass needle."

"Aloha, maybe you're not supposed to act yet," Jake said.

"I have to do something. She's best my friend. I can't sit back and do nothing."

"Call it a hunch, but I don't think you'll be waiting long. But you need to be prepared to wait in case that's what happens. Just be patient," Jake told him.

"I can't." Aloha tore at his hair.

"Why are you acting like you have to do this all alone?" Huron asked.

"Because I'm the tide swooner. I should be able to do something."

"You said it yourself: we don't know where to start. We have no idea what we're facing here," Huron reminded him.

"I just want her back."

"You need to trust God," Jake said.

Aloha ignored him. It's my fault, he thought. I shouldn't have left her alone. He fell to the ground, beating his fists against the dirt. Tails came up, nuzzling him. He barked twice and whined. Huron's eyes widened. Aloha glanced up at him, silently asking what Tails had said.

"He said that God has never abandoned you, and He never will. We will find a way."

Aloha nodded. He closed his eyes and got up off the ground.

"On *whom* do you think we've been depending all this time?" Jake added.

Aloha's eyes widened. That's like after our parents died, and I found Mari. I felt so alone, like I had nowhere to turn, he thought, but then I met Huron and Jake and found a new home. He recalled their crazy adventures and smiled. Jake's right, God has never let us down.

"You're right. I just hope Kiro remembers that." Aloha's eyes lit up. "Hey, wait a minute," he said, looking at Huron. "Do you think you might be able to pick up Kiro's scent as a wolf?"

"My sense of smell is stronger than Tails'. It's worth a shot, but I haven't gone wolf in a while. I'm not sure I still can," Huron said.

"But you'll try, right?" Aloha asked.

"Sure." He closed his eyes and let out a howl. A spiral of faint yellow light encircled him, and he transformed. He grinned. "I can't believe I forgot how awesome this is."

"Focus, Huron," Jake said.

Huron squinted at him. "This from the king of scatter-brained."

"Hey, I got the degree, didn't I?" Jake retorted.

"Knock it off, you two," Mari snapped.

Huron began sniffing around. He went over the same areas Tails had. At first, he caught no scent of her beyond where Tails had lost it. Aloha wrung his hands, waiting.

Kiro moaned in her sleep, hearing her mom tell her, "You've got to stop carrying around that anger. Let it go. Sometimes, love just isn't enough. My past and your father's, well, they caught up to us, and we couldn't get beyond that. I pray that you never let that happen to you."

Even in her dream, she felt the overwhelming force of her guilt. She should never have gotten angry at her mom for what happened. She awoke, sweating as she noticed that Barrett's fire was hotter than ever. Her mother had been so hurt by her anger. I made her cry, she thought. She sat up, feeling worthless to everyone. I belong here, she told herself, because I only cause everyone else misery.

Somewhere in the apocalyptic gloom of the bushes, a pair of shifty eyes glowed brightly. Soon, Barrett thought, very soon, you will be mine.

"Kiro," a voice called to her from her memory, sounding very familiar. Was it her father's voice? "Kiro, get off the ground. I know you're stronger than this. You have to be, and so do I. We all do. So come back to me."

Suddenly she saw Aloha, his hands cupping the sides of her face, and she felt him push her to carry on. She smiled in the darkness in spite of herself. Gradually, she drifted back to sleep. Barrett uttered a low growl, infuriated that she was proving difficult to turn.

Aloha was about to say something when Wolf-Huron clamped his mouth shut. A low growl issued from the back of his throat. His lips curled up, revealing his fangs.

"Huron, what is it?" Aloha asked.

"I smell something evil. Kiro's scent ends where this one begins. I think we should follow it."

Aloha nodded. "Mari, ready your sword. We're going deep into Eden by the looks of it. We'll have to cut through the overgrowth."

Mari held up his sword. "Gotcha."

"Tails, you have to stay here," Huron said.

Tails whimpered.

"Sit."

Tails sat.

"Now stay."

Tails obeyed, watching them leave with worried eyes. The three boys followed Huron through the trees into the mess of tropical plants. Huron had his tail between his legs. His ears twitched at sounds the others could not hear. As they traveled deeper into the forest, Aloha felt a change in the atmosphere. There was a crushing pressure, a weight to the air. The trees and plants shimmied in the gentle breeze, but instead of giving him the peaceful feeling of a lazy summer afternoon, it sent a chill of distress through him. Huron made an abrupt stop. His ears lowered and flattened against the sides of his skull. He uttered a whine as his body shook. The fur on the back of his neck stood up.

"Huron, are you all right? What's wrong?" Aloha asked.

"I can smell Kiro, but whatever is giving off that evil scent is also present. Whatever this thing is, it definitely has her. We better be careful."

Huron paused at a patch of bunched-up plants. Mari and Aloha hurried forward, hacking a path through the weave of vegetation. It was slow work. Their hands were cramping, but they kept at it. At last, they got through. Huron and Jake followed then Huron continued tracking Kiro.

As they traveled on, Aloha began shouting, "Kiro, where are you?"

Kiro woke with a jolt. She could swear that she had just heard Aloha calling for her. She strained to hear him. Only silence returned her inquiry. "Guess I was wrong. I have to get out of here," she told herself.

She didn't think she'd be able to escape, but anything was better than waiting for Barrett to return. She stalked off in a random direction, struggling through the brambles and knots of overgrowth. When she worked her way to a clearing, she began to sprint and noticed the trunk of a palm tree split in half. Weird, she thought, it's cut perfectly in half. She continued forward. She could feel her leg muscles flexing and becoming taut, then releasing the tension and stretching. Her feet pushed off the ground.

After a few minutes, she happened to glance to the side. Before something in her periphery caught her eye, she neglected to pay attention to the scenery. She had focused on speed, just as she would if she were on a racetrack. But now, she stopped dead. What the heck is going on, she thought. The background wasn't moving at all. There was the tree split in half right on the side, just like it had been when she started. In disbelief, she started running again, this time watching the tree. Even as she moved forward, nothing else did. It was like she was running in place.

No way. She blinked, and suddenly the surroundings were different. She looked back and saw that now the broken tree was way behind her. I don't get it, she thought. She ran for ten more minutes before coming to another bad patch of tangled plants. Panting, she pushed her way through the ferns and tropical underbrush and gaped. She saw a rock with fire burning on it. I'm back where I started, but how, she wondered. With a grunt of determination, she jetted off in a different direction. Five tries later, she ended up back at the rock yet again.

"How am I going to get out of here?"

Glaring at her surroundings, she decided to try one last time. This time instead of going straight out from the clearing, she would zigzag around in the forest until she found herself somewhere different. Soon she collapsed, exhausted.

"I'll never get out of here." She rested awhile and then trudged on. At last she approached another clearing, but everything still looked the same.

"I better not be back at the same clearing," Kiro threatened. She had no idea whom she was menacing.

She came through the bushes and the long grasses and found herself in what appeared to be a maze bordered by dead trees tightly grown together. But that's impossible, she thought, because those trees would have died long before they grew together like that. Nevertheless, there it was. She turned to go back through the clearing and discovered behind her another wall of the maze. She kicked it. It was solid. She tried to scale it. She couldn't get a grip. It was too slippery.

As she traversed the maze, her anger at the situation increased with each step. Hitting several dead ends, she decided to wing it and sped off. What seemed like hours later, she could barely move and was making her way slowly along the path, not even trying anymore, when a growling noise stopped her dead in her tracks. She turned and looked over her shoulder, but nothing was there. The growling kept getting louder. Kiro wasted no time. She burst forward with newfound energy. She glanced to her right to see if anything was there, but as far as she could tell, nothing was. Her foot caught on a root that lay on the path. She stumbled and went sprawling. Her chest hit the ground, knocking the wind out of her. Her face rubbed into the dirt and burned. Her lip had been cut open. Tears formed in her eyes as she passed out. When she awoke, Barrett stood above her.

"Having fun, are we?" He sneered at her.

"Where have you taken me?" she cried.

"I haven't taken you anywhere. We're inside your mind. All these images and dead ends are your creations, not mine. Shall I take you back to Eden?"

She glared at him. "Just wait until Aloha gets here. He'll wallop you."

"Please. I will never be brought down by a child. I am the source of all evil. And do spare me the flimflam about how he'll arrive in time to save you. You are mine," he bragged.

Kiro balled her hands into fists. She'd finally had it with him. She got up and kicked him right in the midsection. With a snarl, he slashed his claws across her face. Kiro went down, and he sliced at her side. She got up again, glowering.

"What do you want with me?" she yelled.

Barrett laughed. "You are weak. You can't stand against me. Soon you will break, and then you will be my servant."

"Not that easy," she said as she tried to kick him again. He grabbed her outstretched leg and twisted it, causing her to fall again. She hit her head and lost consciousness again. She woke up briefly to see that she was back at the clearing with the rock and the fire then she was out again.

"I think there's a clearing ahead," Mari called to Aloha as he cut through more branches, bushes, and vines.

"Good," Aloha responded.

It was now early evening. He and Mari were very sore. Huron was behind them panting right along with Jake. I'll bet they're tired of running, Aloha thought. They finally got through to the clearing. As they emerged from the shrubbery, they spotted a fire. The fire was burning on top of a rock. A figure lay sprawled at the base of the rock. Kiro, Aloha cried inwardly. The boys hurried over to her.

"She's unconscious," Huron stated.

"It looks like she's hurt," Jake said.

Aloha knelt beside her, peering at her. There was a scratch on her face and on her side, and her lip was bleeding. "Oh, Kiro, no." He shook her. Her eyes opened.

"Aloha? Is it really you?" She sat up and grabbed him. He hugged her back.

"Hi," he whispered hoarsely.

"We are so glad we found you," Mari said.

Kiro looked up. "Mari, Jake," she exclaimed. Her eyes landed on Wolf-Huron, and she screamed and threw herself into Aloha's arms.

She had him in a death grip. "Kiro," he said in a raspy voice, "can't breathe."

"It's okay," Huron explained softly, "it's me, Huron."

Kiro released Aloha, who gulped in air. "Huron? How can you be a wolf? I must've hit my head harder than I thought."

"No, you didn't. I can turn into a wolf," he replied.

Kiro's eyes widened. "Oh, that's right. Aloha told me about that when he explained about Mari."

"Yeah. I can see why you'd get freaked, though, since you've never actually seen me as a wolf."

"Kiro, what happened to you?" Aloha asked.

"It's Barrett," Kiro whispered. "He brought me here shortly after you left."

Aloha's lips quaked. "What," he yelled.

Kiro shrank from the anger in his voice. He looked at her apologetically. "I'm sorry I left you, Kiro."

"Why're you sorry? I was the one who told you to go. I really wanted you to stay, but I didn't know how to say that."

Aloha blushed. I am an idiot, he thought. Jake, Mari, and Huron, looked away. Aloha suddenly remembered that he and Kiro were not alone. "Where is Barrett now?"

"I don't know. He kept disappearing and then coming back, like he was waiting for something." She proceeded to explain what had happened since she'd been taken. Her friends were agog.

"When I find that guy," Aloha threatened.

An unexpected gust of wind blew violently through the trees, extinguishing the fire on the rock. The shadows deepened, as if a portent of things to come. Aloha inhaled sharply.

Before anyone could move, a demonic voice imposed. "You'll do what, you little pipsqueak?"

"Barrett," Kiro whispered. A shudder passed through her.

Aloha and his brothers turned toward the voice. A shrouded figure stood before them. Get a load of those antlers, Mari thought.

Aloha's lips formed a thin line of disdain. "So you're the one I've been waiting for," he snapped.

The creature drew himself up to his full height. He towered over Aloha by at least a foot and a half. Unfazed, Aloha eyed him, ablaze with anger.

"Ah, yes, tide swooner," croaked Barrett.

"Why'd you take Kiro?" Aloha demanded.

"She is conflicted and weak. Such individuals are easily enslaved."

"You don't own her, pal," Aloha said.

"Oh, I quite disagree. She is mine."

"Yeah? By whose authority," challenged Aloha.

"By my own," Barrett countered.

"Oh, I disagree," Aloha retorted.

"I see we've come to an impasse. You won't take her without a fight," Barrett snarled.

"I'm going to destroy you," Aloha said with a hiss.

Barrett's face swarmed with a smarmy expression. "You're going to do what? You couldn't even stop me from taking her. Face it, you failed her."

Aloha stopped. His eyes widened. Kiro watched him and said, "Don't listen to him."

Aloha lowered his head. "He's right. I did let you down. I should have realized you wanted me to stay with you earlier," he admitted.

"I already told you it was my fault. Snap out of it."

Aloha jerked his head up. "Come on, Barrett, let's get this over with."

Barrett's eyes became resplendent. He opened his mouth and let out a roar.

"Go get him, Aloha," Kiro cheered.

What am I, chopped liver, Mari thought. He came up next to Aloha and put a hand on his shoulder. Aloha looked at him and grinned, raising an eyebrow. Jake and Huron moved protectively in front of Kiro.

"Look around you, tide swooner. There is no water, thus your powers are useless here," Barrett reminded.

Aloha gulped but remained steady. A flash of insight came to him as the fiend continued. Father, come and have your way, he prayed.

"You foiled my servant Shakoda, but I'm glad you took care of that pesky Razzmatazz for me. You have earned my gratitude, but I shall still have to kill you. With you out of the way, I can take over the ocean and make myself ruler of the aquatic world. I shall lead these creatures astray and make them call me king. They will forget their rightful ruler—Most High God—and see only me. Thus, the first act of vengeance will begin."

Aloha and Mari looked at each other and laughed. "Dude, that'll never work."

Barrett ignored them and went on, "I'll strike God at the source of life: water. That's the first blow. Then I will manipulate His stupid human beings into following me as well. All manner of life shall bow before me and call me their Most High."

"Why wouldn't you just try to rule the humans and leave the sea animals alone?" Aloha demanded.

"It's really an adding insult to injury thing," Barrett stated.

Aloha held up his sword. Mari raised his as well. "Let's do this," Aloha said.

"Hmmm, how can you fight with no water to help you?"

"That's what you think." He pulled his hands together as though he were drawing something to him and released a blast of water at Barrett.

"How were you able to do that?" Barrett asked.

"There's a lot of moisture in the air, plus the dew on the plants."

Barrett leaned back for a moment. As he came forward, he opened his mouth wide. Aloha and Mari saw something orange and bright at the back of his throat.

"He has fire breath," Kiro shouted.

Jake and Huron yanked her out of the way. Aloha and Mari jumped aside as Barrett released a stream of fire.

"Jake, Huron, get Kiro out of here and keep her safe," Aloha commanded.

"Right," Jake said.

He had to drag her, because she tried to break free and run back toward Aloha. Huron came up from behind and shoved her forward. As they were attempting to escape, Barrett blew fire at them. Aloha raised his arms and summoned another blast of water to shield them. As he extracted the water from the plants, some of them began to wither and die. He took no notice as he watched Jake, Kiro, and Wolf-Huron disappear through the forest. Aloha went after Barrett, who moved too quickly for him, and knocked the sword from his hands.

Mari reached for Aloha's sword. Barrett breathed his fire onto the sword. It turned red hot and gave off an iridescent orange glow. Mari backed off. He looked from Aloha to Barrett. Aloha was flabbergasted. Mari charged at the monster, the blade of his sword aimed straight out in front of him. Barrett grabbed the end of the blade as he neared. Little drops of blood appeared between his fingers as he swung the sword and Mari to his right. Mari stumbled and fell to the ground. His grip on the sword collapsed, and it clattered to the ground beside him.

"Mari," Aloha cried.

Barrett turned back to him, a wicked grin on his face. He opened his mouth and spat fire at Aloha. Aloha raised another wall of water to extinguish the fire streaming toward him. Grunting in frustration, Barrett whirled around and lunged at Mari. His mouth dropped open, and scorching flames leapt out. Mari rolled away from the flames, snatching up his sword in the process. The flames lit the grass on fire momentarily then burned out. He got up.

"Aloha," he called, "shield me with water."

Aloha formed another water shield in front of Mari. Barrett tried to run behind Mari, but Aloha matched his movements. Sinister hissing filled the air as the flames hit the water and fizzled out. Mari closed the gap between him and Barrett. Barrett exhaled a huge blast of fire, trying to penetrate the shield. Aloha drew more water from the plants and thickened the shield. Barrett snapped his jaws, enraged. Then he reached out, trying to grab Mari.

Mari ducked under Barrett's outstretched arms and plunged his sword deep into Barrett's side. Barrett groaned in agony. He extended his claws and swiped them at Mari. His arm went through the water with ease and sliced across the side of Mari's neck.

"Ah!" Mari shouted.

Oh no, Mari, Aloha thought. He ran behind Barrett, who grabbed Mari by the throat. Aloha managed to keep the water shield in place as he rushed toward the beast. Barrett saw him coming and dropped Mari. He reeled toward Aloha and shoved him back, expectorating more flames. As he did this, Mari stabbed him again, this time driving his sword into Barrett's back. Jerking his sword out of Barrett, Mari saw Aloha land hard on the ground. He looked dazed. Mari dodged the distracted villain and hurried to his brother's side. Barrett bleated with pain and fury. Father, Aloha pleaded, we need your help. How do we beat him?

"Aloha?" Mari asked as he pulled him up.

As Mari was helping him, the answer came to him. Thank you, Father. Please help us to pull this off, fight for us. Aloha looked at his brother. "Mari, I have an idea. Can you distract him?"

Mari gaped. "I can try."

"I'm not going to be able to shield you this time," Aloha said.

"Then I'll just have to be careful," Mari replied. With that, he raced over to the yowling beast. "Hey, you."

Barrett looked at him, his face contorted with wrath.

"Come on, you cretin," Mari hollered, "try to get me."

Barrett leaned back to discharge more fire at Mari, but all that came out was smoke. Barrett made a gargling sound and rushed at him. Mari sidestepped him.

"Can't catch me, I'm the gingerbread man," he yelled.

Meanwhile, Aloha found his sword. It still radiated an incandescent orange. Aloha raised up another small burst of water. He applied it to the handle of his sword. At first the handle sizzled and appeared to shimmer. Then it slowly regained its natural color. The blade of the sword remained red hot. Aloha tapped the handle cautiously with one finger. It seemed cool enough. He tested it, tentatively wrapping his fingers around it. Cool to the touch, he thought, now we're cooking.

He hefted the sword up, careful not to get the blade near him. Heat wafted at him from it. He glanced at Mari, who was still outrunning Barrett. Aloha crept toward the fiend. When Barrett had Mari cornered and was just about to strike, Aloha drove the hot blade into his back all the way up to the hilt. It went through his skin and muscle as easily as a knife through butter. Barrett echoed an inhuman growl of agony. Aloha twisted his sword around, gutting the beast. Putrid smells arose from Barrett's charred insides as the blade's incredible heat cooked his organs. Barrett fell to his knees, rasping his last, rattling breaths. He glared up at the tide swooner.

"It is finished," Aloha said.

"For now," conceded the fiend. "You can only hold me for a time, tide swooner."

"When my master comes, he will end your reign."

An expression of stupefied amazement and understanding came into the monster's eyes. Finally, he died. Aloha turned his back on Barrett, but Mari gawked as chains appeared all over the beast's body. Aloha heard him gasp, and he looked back over his shoulder. He saw the chains fastening themselves around the body. Once he was fully bound, a pit opened up beneath him, and Barrett was swallowed by the earth. Thank you for your defeating him, Father, Aloha prayed.

"Whoa," Mari said.

Aloha approached him, examining the wounds on his neck. "These cuts aren't that deep. You got really lucky."

"Yeah, yeah. So did you, silly. We better get going. Don't wanna be late for Kiro's party."

"Right. Mari?"

"Yeah?"

"Um, thanks," he said sheepishly.

Mari broke into a grin, tousling his hair. "What are big brothers for?"

When the two of them arrived at the beach, Kiro scrambled to Aloha and hugged him. He hugged her back. Huron, who had turned back into a human, Jake, and Tails greeted them eagerly. Tails jumped on the two of them, wagging his tail and licking them ferociously. Mari and Aloha laughed.

"We better get you home, Kiro," Aloha said, a twinkle in his eye.

She squinted at him. Why does it seem like he's being sneaky, she wondered. "All right. I'm sure we could all use a little time away from Eden," she answered.

"Here, Kiro, hold still," Aloha said as he put his hands on the sides of her face.

"What're you doing?" she asked.

"I'm healing your wounds," he explained as he ran his hands over the scratch on her face and her cut lip. Kiro blushed when he his fingers touched her lips. Aloha pretended not to notice and moved his hands to the scratch in her side. "There. All done."

"I feel much better. Thanks."

"Hey," Mari chimed in, "what about my wound?"

"Oh, right. Sorry," Aloha said awkwardly as he healed Mari's neck.

Soul Mates

Tails led the way across the bridge. Kiro was last, and Aloha was ahead of her. They lagged behind the others.

"Hey, we're gonna head off. Okay?" Huron said.

"Oh, sure," Aloha said.

He kept looking over his shoulder at Kiro.

"What? I'm not gonna disappear."

"Man, I am never leaving you somewhere alone ever again."

She smiled. At last, he turned around to face her, walking backward, eyes never leaving her face.

"Well, now you're just being paranoid."

He turned around again, laughing. As they reached the middle of the bridge, he stumbled and lost his balance, pitching sideways as he fell. His legs slid off the boards, and he grabbed at the planks, but his hands slipped on the slick surface. He looked down in horror at the jagged rocks poking up from the waters beneath them. He bent his knees and swung his legs upward to avoid them. Kiro ran forward, grabbed him under the arms, and hauled him up. He fell backward into her lap as they landed. Aloha looked up in surprise. The bridge swayed under them for a minute. Once it stopped, he smiled and said, "Happy birthday, Kiro."

She tousled his hair. "So now I get you as a present? Come on, get up, you."

"I'm trying."

"You know, tide swooner, I know you could have used your power to help yourself. Why didn't you?"

"Uh, didn't think of it."

"Mm. Right."

"In all seriousness, I think I'm too exhausted from the fight."

Her scrutinizing gaze softened. "Thank you for rescuing me."

"You're welcome. I'll just put it on your tab."

She shoved him playfully. He raised his eyebrows, feigning offense as he got up.

"Aloha?"

"Mm?"

"Told you that you'd knock that creep into oblivion," she reminded, grinning madly.

"You called it," he agreed.

Soon they reached her house. When the two of them entered the backyard, everyone came rushing out the back door. They carried gifts and balloons and set them on the patio table. Kiro watched in amazement, stunned by the surprise party. Her mom came out and, to her astonishment, so did her dad. He's here, she thought, running to him. He hugged her tightly.

"I've missed you, kiddo. Sorry I've been so busy with work. With all the traveling, I just got your letters, and they were great. I wish I'd been home to get them sooner. I would have written back. Happy fifteenth birthday."

"Dad, I love you so much."

"I love you too."

"But I thought you weren't coming?" she inquired.

"I was supposed to work, but they changed my schedule at the last minute."

"I see." Her heart leapt. So he had wanted to see her after all.

It was a delightful party. After she opened presents, everyone went in for ice cream and cake. Aloha stopped her. As they stood there on the patio, Aloha extracted a small box from his pocket and said, "Here, for you."

Kiro opened it eagerly. Her eyes widened as she beheld a watch in a blue leather wristband.

"Oh, wow, this is so cool."

"It suits you," he said as she put it on.

"Thank you so much. I love it."

"Yeah, well, you're my best friend and all."

She threw her arms around him. "You're mine, too."

"Uh, Kiro?" Aloha shuffled back and forth on his feet.

"Yeah?"

"Would you, uh, wanna meet me tomorrow morning for a surf?"

"Okay."

An uncomfortable silence fell between them. It seemed that they were struggling to find the words to say to each other. As he turned to leave, he saluted.

"Don't you want to join everyone for cake?" she asked.

"Nah. Not hungry. Besides, someone has to take Tails home."

"Thanks for coming to get me."

"You're welcome. Tell my brothers I'll meet them at home."

"Sure you don't want to stay?"

Her eyes were begging him to stay.

"I'd rather meet you in the morning. Then we can be alone." He gulped as he realized how that sounded. Well, she understood, right? He was about to correct himself, but the smile on her face stopped him. Whatever makes her happy, he thought.

A Year Later

Aloha and Kiro were on the beach. He stood in the darkness, peering at her. Lately, he could not stop thinking about her. She was that lovely age of sixteen, and he got a funny feeling of nerves whenever she was around, even though they'd been almost inseparable for the last five years. He sighed with delectation, lost in her green eyes.

Her breath caught in her throat as she noticed the way his blue-green eyes lit up when he looked at her. He's gotten so handsome, she thought with a self-conscious swipe of her eyes across his face. She was content just to be near him. But he was so distracted lately, hardly talking and jumpy when she did, that they spent most of the time in silence. It was a pleasant but awkward silence, and she wanted to ask him what was bothering him, but she didn't have the nerve. Whatever it was, he wanted to deal with on his own.

She had admitted her true feelings for him to herself after he saved her from Barrett; but since Aloha always politely but firmly turned down every girl who asked him out, she was afraid to ask him for a date. In her opinion, most of those girls were better looking than she. He would never want to go out with me, she decided.

"So, Aloha, how's Jake doing? I heard from Huron that he's gotten accepted to perform on Broadway. Is that true?"

"Huh? Oh, yeah. Mom and Dad are really proud of him." He grimaced, his stare burning into her. Why'd she ask about Jake? Does she secretly like him?

"Oh, that's nice," she said absently.

His intense gaze was making her nervous. Is he angry at me, she wondered. What did I do?

She must not like him that way, Aloha realized, suddenly reassured. And why did he care anyway? She relaxed when she saw his expression soften.

"Yeah," Aloha said. "Jake's pretty smart. And so are Mari and Huron. I don't know how I'm going to compete."

Is he serious, she thought. "Aloha," she said. Her hand was on his arm, sending an electrifying jolt up the back of his spine. "You don't need to compete. You're extraordinary. Why would you want to be any different?"

The timid way she expressed this to him made his heart skip a beat. He moved forward and put his hands on her shoulders, grasping them lightly. He brought his face closer to hers. Without realizing what he was going to do, he closed his eyes and kissed her gingerly. She looked up, taken aback, but her eyes soon closed, and she returned his kiss. *I can't believe he just kissed me*, she thought, elated as they parted, blushing.

Why did I just do that, Aloha wondered, panicked.

"Aloha—"

"I, uh, have to go. See ya," he yelled, running as fast as he could from her.

He knew she could catch him easily if she wanted; she was the fastest runner on the track team. He ran all the way to Eden, hoping against hope that he'd be lucky and catch Mari. He liked to go there straight off when he visited for the summer. Aloha hoped he was still there.

Utterly confused, Kiro realized that he must not feel the way she did. But what on earth had made him kiss her? She shook her head, putting it off as a mistake. For a long time, she couldn't move. Eventually, she sank to her knees.

Aloha stood on the rope bridge calling breathlessly for Mari.

Mari showed up a moment later. "Hello, sailor."

Relieved, Aloha said, "Hey."

"What's wrong? You look as though you've just seen toast," Mari said, making Aloha moan. He never did have a knack for correctly remembering expressions.

Aloha shook his head. "It's just that something happened with Kiro, and I—"

Mari's concern melted into amusement. "Oh," he guessed with a huge smile, "so you finally kissed her, did you?"

"What? How did you know that?"

"Duh. You've had that sappy I'm-in-love look on your face every time you've looked at her for the past year." He put a hand lightly on Aloha's arm.

"I-I have?"

"Oh man, don't tell me you hadn't noticed. I mean, it's pretty obvious to me from watching your dazed, distracted expressions. Hasn't Kiro figured that out yet?"

"No. I mean, I don't think so. Oh man," he said.

"What?"

"It didn't dawn on me that I, like, had a crush on her. I always just thought we were friends."

"Yes, but sometimes friendship grows into love."

"Yeah, maybe. Uh-oh," he cried.

"What!?"

"I just kind of ran from her, Mari. I better go find her."

"You ran from her? I've heard of people doing some dumb things while they've been in love, but that is utterly ridiculous." Mari cracked up laughing, even though he sympathized with both Kiro and his bewildered brother. Aloha left before he got a chance to explain that she also liked him.

Aloha was breathing hard by the time he neared the spot where he'd left her. He expected her to be gone; but as he came toward her, he saw her on her knees, crying. He whispered her name. She looked up, alarmed, and quickly wiped the tears from her eyes.

"Aloha," she stammered.

"Kiro, I need to talk to you."

"What were you thinking when you kissed me?"

"Um, I was thinking of you. It's just, I had no idea that I was falling—uh, that I had a crush on you. I'm sorry. I never thought about it. It just kind of happened. I didn't mean to run away, but I was scared and needed advice." They both blushed for a moment.

"Where did you go?" She raised an eyebrow.

"I went to find Mari. And boy, did he laugh at me for being such an idiot. I guess I deserved it, huh?"

"No," she said. "But next time, I think it would be wise if we talked things out together."

"You're right."

"You know something, Aloha?"

"What?"

"I could have easily caught you," she whispered with a smart grin as she moved closer to him.

He put his arms around her. "Yeah, I know."

Sixteen Years Later

Aloha and the others grew up, as is the way of the world. He became a teacher, the perfect occupation for someone so wise. He also did a smart thing and married Kiro. They were blessed with a son, whom they named Quinn.

Epilogue

Somewhere in the deep cerulean night, a wolf with wavy purple hair and one that looked like a Keeshond raced through a Minnesota forest. Huron stopped when the two of them had put some distance between themselves and his brothers. He sat down. Tails sat beside him, panting. A sly, knowing grin stretched across the wolf's muzzle. Huron looked at him, eyes narrowed.

"Tails, something's been bothering me," he said.

"What is it, friend?" inquired the wolf.

Huron looked away for a moment, then whispered, "I'm even not sure how to ask this, but how can you still be alive?"

Tails' grin broadened, adding a touch of gentleness to his wise face. "Sometimes things happen in the blink of an eye, and sometimes it takes centuries. Wisdom grows with the ages. Some things are not meant to be understood today. We must just be grateful for the time we have together."

"I see," Huron replied. He didn't know what Tails meant exactly, but he had an idea. Although his question hadn't been answered to his satisfaction, somehow he felt fulfilled. Excitement coursed through him. "Come on, boy. Let's find the others."

"As you wish, friend," Tails said.

The two of them ran back toward the ones they had left. Aloha and his son were busy racing up a dirt hill next to a bluff. "Quinn," Aloha called, looking back over his shoulder.

"Yeah, Dad?"

"Try it this way," he said. Aloha leapt into the air.

His son followed, saying, "Up and out."

They soared above the trail they had been running. Aloha followed the corkscrewing path, flying close to the ground. As Quinn traced the hill low in the air, he touched his hands down on the ground and exclaimed, "Look, Dad, I can walk on my hands."

Aloha nodded, a smile of approval on his face. Then they spurted upward. When they cleared the trees, they saw Jake and Mari on a winding road that ran right next to the woods. Aloha and Quinn headed over. The four greeted each other with a nod. Out of nowhere, Huron, changing back into a human, burst through the trees. He winked as he flashed by. Quinn squealed with delight. He saw Tails chasing after them, barking from below. Huron swooped down and grabbed him. He flung the wolf into the air so that he was flying too. Tails whined as he started to fall, and Aloha caught him. He wiped his hand across the wolf's brow and said, "Leap and fly with us, Tails."

Tails sprung out of his arms and into the air, wagging his tail as he flew.

"Yay," Quinn shouted.

"Well, look who's having all the fun," came a voice.

They looked over to see Kiro wearing a patient smile. Aloha blushed. He'd forgotten all about the fireworks. The sky had done that to him; the stars had bewitched him.

"I'm sorry, Kiro."

"I'm sorry too, Mom," Quinn whispered.

She let out a gentle chuckle. "It's okay. This is a much better way to see the fireworks, anyway."

Everyone agreed as they swam through the night sky, basked in glittering light from the rain of colors. Monochromatic rainbows dashed across their faces. *Heartical, forever our journey,* Aloha thought with a smile.

www.ingramcontent.com/pod-product-compliance
Lightning Source LLC
LaVergne TN
LVHW011939070526
838202LV00054B/4726